Praise for the Work of Paul Lisicky

About *The Burning House*

"...took hold of me from the first page and I read it straight to the end. There is a compulsive forward movement to the story that makes it feel like a mystery—except the enigma here has to do with the different attractions of the beautiful sisters, Joan and Laura, and the allure of the old seaside town. It's the sort of very good book that makes you feel like you're dreaming when you're reading it, and opened-up and curious when you finish. So much happens, each word counts. I really loved it"

—Alice Elliott Dark

"...an achingly lovely novel about the things that bind us together in this life and the things that pull us apart. Paul Lisicky has an extraordinary gift for exploring emotional nuance and the rhythms of desire. With this book he yet again asserts himself as one of the select writers who continues to teach me about the complexities of the human heart."

—Robert Olen Butler

About *Lawnboy*

"Quite simply, the real thing, a novel of mystery and great beauty. The appearance of a writer like Paul Lisicky—a writer who deeply respects the complexities of love and desire, who can find tragedy and transcendence almost every where he looks—is a rare event"

—Michael Cunningham

"Lisicky's prose shines, at times hilarious, at others entrenched in sorrow and longing, but always gorgeous to read...The reconciliations between the characters are moving and earned, graced with compassion and vitality."

—Bret Anthony Johnston

"Nobody writes about hilarious longing the way Paul Lisicky does. Some writers manage to be funny and sad in turn...Lisicky manages to be both at the same time."

—Elizabeth McCracken

ALSO BY
PAUL LISICKY

Lawnboy
Famous Builder

THE BURNING HOUSE

PAUL LISICKY

Etruscan Press
Wilkes University
84 West South Street
Wilkes-Barre, PA 18766

 WILKES UNIVERSITY

www.etruscanpress.org

Library of Congress Cataloging-in-Publication Data

Lisicky, Paul.
The burning house : a novel / by Paul Lisicky.
     p. cm.
ISBN 978-0-9819687-8-0 (pbk.)
I. Title.
PS3562.I773B87 2011
813'.54--dc22

                              2011005678

First Edition
11 12 13 14 15 5 4 3 2 1

Design by Michael Ress

THE BURNING HOUSE

A Novel

PAUL LISICKY

etruscan press

For Denise Gess,

In memory

There is a way
if we want
into everything
—MICHAEL DICKMAN, "My Autopsy"

Acknowledgments

Portions of this novel appeared in *The East Hampton Star, Ecotone, Hunger Mountain, fwriction*: review, *The Literary Review, NANO Fiction,* and in the anthology *A Book for Daniel Stern* (Sheep Meadow Press). An earlier version of the opening paragraph appeared as the poem "The Night in Question" in *Verse Daily.* Outtakes from the novel appeared in *Prairie Schooner* (as "Bess Helen's Dog") and *Le Petit Journal* (as "Lumina Avenue"). The excerpt from "My Autopsy" by Michael Dickman is used by permission of Copper Canyon Press, www.coppercanyonpress.org.

With thanks and love to Denise Gess, Deborah Anne Lott, Elizabeth McCracken, Victoria Redel, and Carol Houck Smith for reading multiple drafts of this book. Thank you to Philip Brady, Robert Mooney, Starr Troup, Marissa Phillips, and everyone at Etruscan Press for their kindness and enthusiasm. Thanks to Jim Cihlar for his precise eye, to Kapo Ng for his fantastic cover.

And to Mark Doty: *light, climbing up the aerial*—Everything.

THE BURNING HOUSE

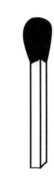

PAUL LISICKY

CHAPTER 1

The rising seas, the sinking lawn: none of that bothered me tonight. Laura's health and mind, shifting like water. Mister Greasy, Son of Unabomber. Far away. Yay. I walked from the bay. I could not see. But I might have been given a fresh brain, inspired and outwardly turned, and as soon as I spoke those words to the deep, I swear creatures started coming toward me. Squirrels, raccoons, deer, herons, catbirds, footfalls on fallen leaves. I was like someone out of a freaking folktale, who knew not death or the churned-up stomach but moved through the night with the lightest tread, changing it with the benevolence of his passing. Oh, I'm exaggerating for effect now, I'll admit it. Real contentment has none of that extremity or loopiness. No sign of endings, or the long black coat creeping out from behind a bush. What was I telling you? It was something like this: the world was made exactly for us and we'd never have to leave it.

•

Laura had told Joan and me not to expect her till midnight. There was accounting to take care of, some missing shipments from Connecticut. Then that little heart-to-heart with Madison, who'd taken to dealing behind the register, silly girl. As if we'd never once think about the parade of big talkers who seemed to show up ten minutes before closing every night.

But trust in my instincts? Well, yes: I still couldn't go in without pulling up the garage door first. Birdseed, garden hose, herbicide, rake tine: empty as could be. No sign of Laura's car. What was it about those smells that always brought me home to myself?

Joan stood inside the living room with her back to the windows. "Are you busy?" I said.

The worst way to start a conversation, *any* conversation: I knew. So much for my practicing what I had to say in my head.

She sat down on the arm of the sofa and gave me that frank stare of hers. I saw Laura in that frank stare, though that's the last thing she'd want to hear right now. Enough comparisons to that older sister, thank you very much. Same sweet crooked mouth, same moist hair falling down her back, same tendency to keep her shoulders raised, as if she had to correct what her posture really wanted to do.

"You're on your way out?" I said.

"Well, I bet if I showed up a little late the meeting would start on time. Wouldn't that be the way things worked?"

"Let's just talk in a few days, then. Saturday? I don't think I have anything to do on Saturday. Is that good?"

"Sure," she said. "As far as I know, I'm free."

My eyes weren't matching my mouth—I felt that. It was as if I couldn't get the whole face to behave. Why?

"Your hand." She squinted a bit, drew closer, and frowned at what she saw. "That hand still looks reddish to me. Is that a rash? Didn't I see you lifting bushes out of the car the other night?"

I shook my head. I pushed my hand in my pants pocket so we could move on to the relevant thing.

That old habit of taking notice—she still held onto that part of herself. It was as central to Joan as blood. She'd always been like that, even when she was younger, studying maps, studying trees, studying birds. But don't ask me how she managed to see two feet in front of her. Bad enough to lose your mother, your apartment, your business, your boyfriend—come on! But having to move in with your sister because *she* inherits your mother's house and you're left with nothing? All in six months' time? I don't think so. Imagine having such shit visited on you when things had been going in your favor, when your life had been humming along like a song. You might just think that your song would keep humming like that forever.

Back then, that kind of absurdity struck me as the way of things. Slip off the dock into the water, and this happens and that happens, one by one by one. And who knows how you got caught inside any of it, as if you're just an integer in one of those terrible logic problems you could never figure out all the way back in math class.

I said, "Does Laura seem different to you?"

The corners of her mouth turned up as if she were about to smile, the kind of half-smile you learn to make when you're used to getting news you're not exactly able to hear. It took her a moment to clear out her head. Then she adjusted herself on the sofa as if she knew she'd be leaning back, arms folded, for a little while. "I wish I could say I thought you were completely out of your mind," she said.

Though a part of me felt calmer, another part of me just didn't know. It would have been easier to hear that I was dreaming up the whole damn thing. Maybe that's what I'd been wanting to hear all along.

What could we say? There wasn't much point in comparing notes. We weren't talking about the obvious: no pains, no shortness of breath. No trouble getting out of bed in the morning—you've heard of people like that. I'm talking about people who stay in bed twelve hours a day, and then it's at least twenty minutes more just to get moving to the bathroom. Honestly, if you didn't know her and saw her walking down the street, you might think, that's one beautiful woman. What is she, two years out of college? Three? What does she do, yoga five times a week? Takes all the right vitamins, avoids the sugar and salt? Dairy and wheat: they don't even get near her, right? But I knew my wife. She was a phenomenon. She worked, she painted, she ran, she swam: she was twenty-seven people in one. Not that she didn't have it in her to be a pain in the ass, but what living thing—human, plant, animal—doesn't every now and then?

"The thing is, she doesn't want to be told what to do. I get that. I completely understand that about Laura. Would I behave that way if I were in her position? Maybe."

"You mean going to the doctor," Joan said. "Getting things checked out."

"Maybe. Or whatever. Maybe it's just my threshold for patience. Maybe I'm just not as patient as I used to be."

"You've talked to her about all that?" Joan said.

"Oh, yeah."

"And she refuses to do anything about it?"

"Well, no. It's not as simple as all that. But a check-up's maybe a little less important than checking her e-mail and maybe a little more important than cleaning out the bird feeder."

"And you don't think she's just taken on too much? A lot's been going on around here." Out came a little laugh, as if she meant to soften her words. "But I don't have to tell you about that."

"I mean I don't like to admit to trouble as much as the next person. Wouldn't I rather just walk around saying things couldn't be better between us? How is my wife? Glorious!"

Out from the lagoon, a low comforting vibration like a snowplow down a street. The most fantastic boat imaginable tried to make it past our neighbor's dock. Lights on the flying bridge, party music in the speakers: the works. I'd say it was three times too wide and long for the channel, easily. It was a dream of an apartment house, lights in the windows, toppled on its side. But the captain wasn't giving in, not yet. He was getting to where he had to go. And the propeller scooped into the bottom, the lovely rich smell of bay mud drifting in through the dew on the screens.

Joan gave a dull, wry look as if she were long past the point of being surprised by anything.

"Maybe I could say something," she said. "Maybe it's easier for a sister than a husband. I could be more casual about it. I could *try* to be."

"What would you say to her?"

"Oh, I don't know. Indirectly. I think that would be the only way to approach things. Let me think about this." Then her face got very intent.

"Just don't let her know that we had this little talk, okay? I think that would freak her out. I think it would freak *me* out."

"Of course not."

I pushed out of my chair. I stood for a second, moving my arms up and down. I couldn't sit still. This spring in my feet, this urge to pick up: where was that coming from? I clapped my hands, once, and waited for her to come to the window, to look for the boat.

"That would be great. That would make me feel so much better."

"Isidore?"

"And everything's okay back in that room? It's so small. I mean, I still think you'd be happier down the hall. You'd have a lot more privacy."

"Oh, that's what you keep saying."

"I'd be glad to help out anytime. Really. Just let me know when, Joan. It's not like I don't have some time on my hands."

"Thank you," she said more gently than I'd expected. "I'm perfectly fine for the moment. Thank you for thinking of me." And she moved her head with one emphatic turn to the left.

With that, she stood. The embrace I expected to happen with ease just felt, what?—weird. It wasn't any embrace. She put a hand upon my back with a sort of steering. I let my arms fall back down before I could close up any space between us. It wasn't the way I usually thought of myself, awkward with someone I'd been close to for seventeen years.

•

I reached for a dust cloth and tackled the dining room. The chair rungs, the floor beneath the computer desk, the hood of the fireplace. Once that cloth was in my hand, the world was all mine. Or should I say "I," "mine," and "me," disappeared, and all that remained was the project of reparation and repair. My cloth turning blacker, me hovering somewhere up above, looking down upon those shining, spacious rooms. None of my failures haunted me from up here—no string of lost jobs, no wrecked cars, no waking up with that fullness in my chest, those drumming words: you'll never do it, you'll never do it, you'll never do it. Even the house itself felt like it had never been Mama's, but ours alone, as if Laura and I had designed the floor plan ourselves. It didn't even matter that we'd never picked the clocks and bowls, that we'd been too worried to move a thing since the house had been given to us. For in touching them with the cloth, I was recognizing the forgotten. I was refreshing them with promise and light, and, in turn, joining myself to their makers.

I still couldn't believe that we were living in such a place. Sometimes I woke up at night with the voice of Craig Luckland, the cop from down the street, ringing in my eardrum: "There's been a mistake. You have three hours to get out or your stuff will be sent to France."

"Do you mind if I help?" Laura said.

I hadn't known she'd been watching me. Laura stood at the doorway, arms crossed, in a thin, pink Led Zeppelin T-shirt, with tiny holes splitting her sleeve. Always that armful of gorgeous black hair. The question so delighted me I didn't have an answer. These days, I took care of the house. It was the least I could do, now that the accident had put me out of commission, and she was driving forty-five miles each way, in stalled traffic, to run her music shop in Ocean Ridge.

She might as well have told me that she loved the space between my front teeth.

"You look like you're enjoying yourself."

"Just cleaning up."

She walked over to me, kissed the crown of my woolly head and picked up a cloth. "You're not going to fuss if I miss something?" She said it in that voice, that low voice that always got my attention.

"Me? Fuss?"

Life was here again. She'd seemed to be putting some weight back on. Had Joan talked to her about seeing the doctor? I wasn't going to broach it, at least not yet, if only because, why tempt things when the gods, even if it's just for a minute, are all of a sudden on our side? Laura glowed like someone who'd run seven miles up and down the boardwalk and beach, face lifted to the sun. Even I stopped feeling like shit about staying at home. My broken hand was healing, and I knew I'd be back to fixing cars within days, doing the thing that mattered most to me.

We squatted, stood, squatted again. We waxed. We sprayed. We oiled. We scraped. We polished. We worked our cloths in wider and wider arcs, almost sighing when we came upon that space behind the bookcase, the cobwebs so soft they might have been bandages. By the time we looked up, the sky outside the windows had turned eyecup blue. Soon enough we wouldn't be able to see without bringing extra lamps to the room.

"This feels nice," I said.

"It is nice," she answered, eyes concentrating on the tabletop.

"We're always running around. *Everybody's* always running around. What's up with all that? Why are we always so afraid of standing still?"

"Could I ask you a question, honey?"

I folded my cloth over the arm of the chair.

"Has Joan's moving in been stressful for you? It's funny that we've never talked about it. What's it been, like, four months?"

The question was so direct that it stopped me. I didn't know what to do with it. It was like the lost child we'd never have, so stealthy and shy that our indifference to him ashamed us. But I was hardly the one to bring up the issue. On my wages, we couldn't have lived within fifty miles of the bay we loved, and doesn't that sorry truth worm through everything? So Joan had been kicked out of her apartment. So we had the space for her, courtesy of *their* mother? What was I to say to that?

"Well," I said, "I was afraid that it was going to be weird. But it's really turned out for the best. Who would have ever guessed such a thing?"

In truth, I knew that things would never be the same once she moved in with us. I don't care what you say: circumstances like that can bring out the ugliness in people. I'd always loved Joan. I'd always loved the way she'd brought vividness to a room. Even the walls seemed to shiver awake when she passed in front of them. When she was nearby, I'd start to notice things that hadn't caught my eye before: a loose bristle painted into the cabinet, the tall ebony pitcher with the cracked handle. And you could never predict what would come out of her mouth. She seemed determined to lift the screen that made our lives so careful and tidy, and until she sat between us on the sofa, we hadn't known how much we'd been secreting away. I didn't want to lose that. It felt unbearably valuable, of the highest currency; the fact was Joan was still young in a way that we weren't. She had the faith that life could still change. I mean, look: it was no small thing that she was giving up all her spare time to try to stand up against those builders. I wouldn't have seen any of it if she hadn't told me what their project meant for us: filthy water in the lagoons, more cars on the streets. And do you really want to wake up in the morning to silence instead of the birds you're used to taking for granted?

"You never said that you were nervous."

I said, "You're not happy about things?"

"Listen, it's great that she's here. I love her company. I do. She's my sister, for Christ's sake. I didn't know how much I missed her until she moved in with us. It's just—" She pulled in her lips, struggling. "You do sort of seem happier than you've seemed in a long while."

The dimmest memory: a taste of bloodied cotton, the dentist's dry fingers pushing in my mouth. "I don't understand."

Her eyes filled to the lower lid, careful not to spill down her cheeks. Her face stayed perfect, absolutely serene. For a moment, I thought, shouldn't I be the one who's crying here? Until I felt bolder and brighter, like the lamp I'd been holding.

I always thought that we all have a story that we play out, in large and in miniature, through every interaction of our lives. Joan's story was that she'd tried to rescue lost things, only to be left behind by what she thought she'd saved. Laura's was that she'd seek out the brightest fire, only to find her own fuel swallowed up to feed the other. My story? I don't want to sound crude, but if you talked with the highest power, I believe you'd be told that my need to touch and be touched would lead me to hurt the ones I cared about.

What a terrible thing.

That was all I knew. Where else wasn't I stepping outside of myself, listening to how I talked, watching how I moved? Here was generosity. My skin and my soul one and the same, so I didn't have to think about me and my terrible punishing hopes. I was shoehorned into my body, which fit like the finest leather loafer, no rubbing or space behind the heel. And how I was able to walk and walk, as if the world went onward and up, to infinity.

I led her down the hallway, by the hand.

I lay on top of her, weight resting on my elbows. When I held her face between my hands, her mouth parted, the quiet so deep that the world was struck dumb. First the baseboards with their tappings and clicks. Then the currents in the fusebox. The scrub pines, the cardinals, the bulkheads sipping water: they went silent too. Somewhere, at the bottom of the world, a young man churned inside his lover for the very first time, burning up inside the body that enclosed him. And Laura in Mama's bed, already beyond reach.

CHAPTER 2

The new house ate up every square foot of its lot. Copper roofing, copper flashing, copper downspouts: every last detail crying out, *notice me, notice me, keep up with me.* Exactly the kind of house Joan would have despised, with good reason. Dozens of these were sprouting up on street after street, replacing the tidy modern ranch houses on the water. The houses were little, I know. But did anyone these days have a clue they were once sold fully furnished, all the way down to the toothbrush, from the seventh floor model home at Bamberger's, Newark? And even the minister of French culture, invited by builder, Boris Letsky, had a thing or two to say about them: "The higher the satellite, the lower the culture." As if that were the cleverest thing. But look, those ranch houses with their clerestories, open rooms, tongue-and-groove ceilings, and pocket doors were exactly what serious architects were aping these days, even as the dodos in our zone were tearing them down.

At least that's what Joan had made me see.

Just between you and me, though, I had to admit that I loved the new house. Okay, not that I loved it exactly, just that seeing a house like that come together blew out all the fog in my head. All the fog that enabled me to pass through the world without looking. I looked forward to it day upon day. Here was the ugly of it: as long as things were being thrown up around me, I'd never feel stuck in myself.

At my feet, a bumblebee dragged itself across the gravel.

I picked up shards of wood, stuffed my pockets until they were fat with it. This was how I filled the hour after dinner every night except Tuesdays: I walked through the new houses just as the sky went dark. It was my time to be alone, time to be apart from Laura and Joan, who stirred up the rooms they passed through, agitating the air. So much energy between them, energy and nerves, voices stormy, legs impossibly tall and tapered. How could I stop from being lost? I loved them, don't get me wrong. They were excitement; they were beauty to me: a big bright bank of redwoods sparking at the edge of the sky. But sometimes a man needed to know who he was again. I went from one house to the next, standing inside their privacy, their loneliness. Boards aching, smell of dust still hot from the blade. Little shifts like murmurs above my head. So this is how I'll spend the foreseeable, said the pieces of the house. So this is the weight I will carry. And somewhere, deep inside, the memory of the woods where they came from: the dense, mossy thick, three-thousand five-hundred miles away.

"I take it you set your own rules."

A ruddy fellow, a little soft in the belly, trudged up the ramp. I couldn't help but think of some fuming hen, body swaying side to side, head pecking. For some reason, I thought this particularly funny, and I started to laugh before I had the chance to explain.

"What's up?"

"I take it you're not a reader." He pointed to the hand-lettered sign on the fence I'd pushed through:

ACTIVE CONSTRUCTION SITE: TRESPASSERS PROSECUTED TO FULLEST EXTENT OF THE LAW.

"You think I'm up to something?"

I kept the reaction from my face, stony and plain. It was a trick I'd taught myself, years back, in the guidance counselor's office, or in front of my moody father just before the thought of spanking me passed over his face.

He raised his chin some. "I do."

"You're asking to pat me down?" I half-turned, held up my arms against fresh drywall. I couldn't get a laugh out of him, though. Instead, the air buzzed as if he were convinced that I wanted to be boned by him.

"How do I know you're not going to come back in an hour, walk out with some pipes and fixtures?"

"You don't." I looked him over without reservation: the orange crew cut, the puckered white star to the right of his nose, as if someone had pushed a screwdriver into his face.

"What's in your pockets?"

I folded my arms, pushed up my biceps with my fists. I used the grin I depended upon when a little charm was in order. "So you really are after me."

"*Fuck* you."

"What makes me think you're going to believe what I say anyway?"

"We've been missing three cords of wood from this property in the last week. A good two thousand dollars' worth in supplies. At least."

"You want to come over to my backyard and check?"

The guy cleared his throat, part awe, part disgust. Nothing like zoning in on the thing he least wanted to hear. To serve it up to him, to force his face in it, and make him eat it on his knees. The dolt. If I truly liked guys, he'd be the last person I'd fool around with. *Try losing that mushy ass, pal,* I wanted to say. *Then maybe someone, woman or man, would want a roll in the hay with you.*

He started swinging his arms freely, a little violence in it, not aimed at any particular target. Was someone going to get hurt? I could take him down, I knew that. I could send him straight to the hospital if that was what he wanted. But the scenario was almost too easy: the thin red drip from the nose, the squint of vulnerability. No golden, molten rage. I'd have rather been blindfolded, force-fed raw chicken with a knife to the throat.

The truth was I hadn't hit anyone since high school. Joe Batschelet, in the far back corner of the library, throwing tiny balls of wet Juicy Fruit at the back of my head. I was skinny back then, half of the weight I am now. In his thickness, Joe had decided that I was a worthy target just because I kept my head down all the time and didn't say a word in class. The bad part wasn't the punch; it was shocking how easily my fist fit into his face. It was as if my whole life had been leading toward that moment: his face, my fist, our marriage. What bothered me was the aftermath. Joe had lost part of his sight in his left eye. And wasn't I reminded of that each time I passed one of his friends in the school hall? They looked at me as if I'd held a sour, curdled secret. And I wanted to say, but I'm not what you think I am. I'm good, I'm good.

Another guy, much taller than the ruddy fellow, walked toward us now. I couldn't see who it was, but the sheer height of him was wonderful to take in. The insides of my bowels froze. And I felt shorter than I'd felt in ages.

"Evening, gentlemen." The police badge he flashed managed to catch the light from the street lamp.

"Craig," I said with a relief too broad, too long.

He wasn't in uniform. Instead, he had on a navy-blue polo shirt that he'd tucked into his jeans to hold the fabric as close as possible to his torso. He looked like he'd been airbrushed in real life, up and off the page. "Someone isn't happy here?"

"The man violated a no trespassing order," Red said.

"The gentleman thinks"—I couldn't stop the smile on my face—"the gentleman thinks I'm here to steal property."

"Oh yeah?"

"And he doesn't think I can read."

Craig Luckland looked at the guy as if he were expecting someone to come out behind a tree to take his picture. He had the kind of face that had always known it was handsome. The man behind that face knew that it could get him anything he wanted. Luckland's love for himself would have enraged me if it hadn't been so weirdly magnetic. Still, it helped no one in town that Luckland had just appeared in a reality show about bachelor cops. Now he couldn't even concentrate without thinking about every lift and turn of that expensive face. The truth was he'd eat off his underpants on another reality show if it ensured his place in front of the camera. But that didn't mean I didn't like the guy.

"We've lost ten thousand dollars this week," Red said.

"And you saw Mirsky stealing something."

"I happened to be walking around the property," Red said.

"I guess I missed the sign," I said, shrugging.

"Well, then," Luckland said.

Then Luckland took him by the arm and drew him aside.

He drew his head to the guy, talking in low, confidential tones, more counselor than policemen. He kept almost aiming his face of great concern and patience at the guy's lesser face, blond-red, with babyish features. It didn't take long for Luckland's eyes to harden. They gave up a shock of raw feeling above the practiced smile. The guy simply wasn't giving him what he wanted. What was it that Craig wanted?

Then I got it: he was waiting to be recognized.

Luckland walked over to me, still smiling, but weary about the eyes, as if the direct challenge to his star power had hit him where he lived. It told him the tale of his fate from here on out: life in our town would never give him what he needed.

"What timing," I said. "What if you hadn't come by? *Shit.*"

We watched Red moving down the street, his walk deliberate and henny. *Buck, buck, buck, buck, buck*, said the walk.

"You're not naked," Craig said, rubbing his shaved chin.

I pictured the corners of my smile held up with pushpins. I asked him what he was talking about.

"You," he said, "you always have your shirt off. Every time I run into you. I'm surprised you even have any clothes in your closet. Do you have clothes in your closet?"

"Is that right?" I felt my expression changing, though I tried to remember the old trick: keep it stony, keep it plain.

"And you're not singing something. Aren't you always singing a little tune?"

"I don't sing."

"As if you don't sing."

"What do I sing?"

"What are you usually singing? 'Born to Run.' Yeah," he said, pleased with his ability to make connections. "That's it."

I tried to reach for something witty, but I came up short. I'd never sung "Born to Run" in my life. At once, I felt that rude, rash desire to get away fast and quick. The deadly effect of standing in the presence of an authority figure whom I was expected to suck up to but couldn't without seeming false, or looking like some totally extinct bird.

We started talking—Laura, Joan, my truck accident, everything you'd imagine. But my mind kept going back to his assessments of me. He hadn't been making fun—I'd have been taking myself too seriously if I'd thought he'd been making fun. But I felt a little crazed. Who wanted to be told that he'd lost the ability to surprise and change, that he'd finally become himself: a man whose two coordinates were his body and his singing? Even as he'd been standing up for me, I knew he saw me as someone who'd never lived up to his potential, an aimless joeboy who'd leave the world without a mark or a stain. Maybe it was all about the effects of that face on me, a face with such magnetizing power that it could pulverize steel, draw water from stone. It said: *I'm embedded in the world, while you're only halfway here. A woman would take me over you any day, and isn't it a sign of the brute injustice of this world that you were born yourself and not me?* In another situation I might have laughed aloud at the absurdity of it, but what if he was right? What if I was already dead and was the last to find out? What if I wasn't fully present enough in my life to give myself memories? No connections made, no ability to sustain a conversation: a phantom, a walking ghost, a Frankenstein monster.

And what about the women I'd loved? What had I given them?

I looked up. I imagined a trash fire inside the corners of an unfinished room until the house was charred.

"I need a job." And it came out with such desperation that I turned my face away. Hot tears roiled in the base of my throat.

Then Craig put his arm around my shoulder and smiled with characteristic concern, as if our rightful places in the grand scheme of things had been assumed.

"I was waiting for you to ask."

•

But I hadn't always been a member of the walking wounded. Once the world had been brighter and alive, rich with incident:

1982. I'm making my way to my high school algebra classroom. A crowd gathers outside the doors of the auditorium. Mrs. Muscufo tries to break it up. Voices are raised, but only a few do as they're told. I'm fourteen. I should keep going—isn't it about time for a pop quiz? Instead, I stand on my toes, flex my calves until they're stopped up with blood. Everyone is tall: eager and greedy and ruthless. There's a sour smell of hot woolens. Why am I here? I can't tell you that. Instinctively, I hate crowds and anything that draws crowds: sports, tournaments. Send me to the outfield, and watch me drop the ball from my mitt, screwing it up for my team. And yet I can't tear myself away. I'm losing precious minutes as my algebra teacher is most likely handing out the pop quiz.

In seconds, I work my way to the front of the crowd so that I'm standing inside the dark vault of the auditorium. The stage itself is drenched with red-gold light. I'm still small; this is years before my arms thickened. There's a piano player hunched over the baby grand. And on the stage, a voice so large that it destroys the girl who's singing. Her body doesn't so much matter anymore: the voice is somehow greater than the body. If the room had been any smaller, I wouldn't have been able to stand it. Too private, too intimate. But she might as well be handing me a chain, pulling me up the side of the highest mountain, link by gorgeous link.

Uptown, going down, old lifeline...

The song punishes as much as it feeds. It comes apart in pieces just as soon as I can pick out a pattern. I'm not sure I even like the song, but that's not exactly the point. It's as if I haven't even known my skin before; it feels stranger, yet more beautiful. I'd always thought my body was mine alone: small and wholly mine and expendable: who would have known that it was a part of something else? I glance back at those who stand behind me. There's Tom Pomeroy, there's Jose O'Neill. Though they're concentrating, they're not as radically changed as I. On a pure animal level, they only know the voice is something they have a duty to hear. God wants it from them, though they wouldn't call it God.

She finishes. I want to get away before she starts the next number, because I know she'll never sound like that again, and I need to preserve it, like something I'd keep in a jar. But I'm wedged in between two people; I can't move without stepping on feet. Someone turns, and then I see her between two heads. She isn't radiant or extraordinary anymore, but she's one of us, a senior. Someone I've seen walking up and down these halls. There's nothing remarkable about her, nothing to write home about her rounded shoulders, her deep-black bank of hair, her height. But her singing tells me something different: she's an old soul, older than anyone I've ever known, including my grandfather.

Walking down faster, walking with the master of time...

Life could still change: that's what her singing told me. She came at a moment when she was exactly what I needed. It wasn't like those were the worst of times. My father hadn't died yet; nor Uncle Moishe or my cousin Danny. Or none of the friends that were to come later. But listening to that bright big sound, I could tell that my life wasn't going to be the neat, predictable shape I'd already pictured. There was no way out of it. The years ahead were going to be hard, harder than I had it in me to imagine. And yet the news didn't make me want to run or curl into myself. Though it took me a year and a half to speak to her, I already knew that we'd share the same house and bed one day. I saw us sitting across from each other in our kitchen, a warm, yellow sun streaming through a part in the curtains, lighting up the table.

The fact of that gave me comfort, and I walked on to algebra, where the teacher, Mrs. Voorhees, didn't seem to care that I was late, and flashed, somewhere beneath the sternness, a look of approval.

CHAPTER 3

I have a job.

I said it to the pitch pines, the violets, and the gravel, though no one was there to hear it. I jogged past the shopping center, the marina, the boats with their pulleys and eyelets. I was telling Laura, Joan—anybody, in my head—that Craig Luckland would see to it that Ferris would take me on as a property manager: one of those guys who checked up on houses while their owners were away. Of course Joan would say, "You're going to work for Ferris? You can't stand Ferris." And she'd be right. Not that I couldn't stand him, but one minute you were his best pal, and the next he'd walk right past you as if he couldn't be bothered. At least a hello, buddy. And is it my fault that you walk through the world like an old man, or at least an old man before his time? But things would change once he got to see how hard I worked. Me, the human tractor.

I'm going to pay off my Visa, and after that, I'm going to buy Laura a new car and dig a water feature!

I laughed aloud like a madman, startling a woman who was hauling out her trash. What supreme, nutty pleasure it was to laugh in the night like a madman!

Our house couldn't have been quieter, though my ears roared. I walked from room to pretty room, fighting off the urge to cry, *I'm here, I'm here,* waving the flags of my good news. Lights burned as if in a stadium. I shut them off, one by one by one, and did twenty pushups on the kitchen floor. Not just everyday pushups, but the kind with a clap in them.

The washing machine churned sloppily, as if glad for its work.

I stood still outside Joan's room, chest banging and large. Light leaked beneath her door. She was talking to somebody, but it wasn't her phone voice. It was higher than usual, less from the chest, in cold clear tones. Maybe she was already talking to Ferris, scoping out the details of my employ. But there was nothing of that familiarity or ease about the conversation. Her voice sounded hard, the syllables slack, as if the roof of her mouth had been scorched.

I miss you terribly, Mama.

Saving a neighborhood . . . what was I thinking?

Things aren't so good here. This is not how I'd pictured my life. (A little laugh.)

Whatever made me think that this would be enough for me?

I stood absolutely still, stolid as a suitcase. I'd never heard anything so lonely and remote. Really, she had every reason to be mad at her mother, and was she mad?

I sat down on the floor, still breathing, head buried on my folded arms. I licked, just once, a patch of my skin.

Years ago I'd seen a fox in the bracken across Route Nine. She had mange; her hair had come off in circles, skin smelly, a deep outrageous pink. We faced each other from a distance of twenty feet, both of us ashamed, both knowing there was no way I could make things better, even as I wanted to. I only had myself here: poor, hulking with excitement and spent dreams. I saw a part of me then—a part of me that I didn't know I possessed—rise up and off my body to put my arms around Joan from behind.

I held her like that, in my imagination, until she stopped talking.

Then the part of me that was my body just had to get out of that house.

•

I lifted the bar above my chest. I'd put on fifty more pounds than I could handle, but why not? I was wired tonight. Little impulses sparkled, crackled like ice chips inside my brain. Burning nurtured my biceps; my axis, throat to furry belly, tensed and vigilant. I couldn't hurt my back again, not now, now that I had a job. Twelve reps, twelve deep breaths. In through the nose, out through the mouth. One, two, three, four, five. . . .

The bar went back on the rack with a clatter.

I sat up quick, too quick. Panting, a little dizzy, winded. It occurred to me that my protein intake was low. Was I dehydrated? Luckily the gym was empty after nine, none of the usual types escaping their wives, slumping on benches, yelling into cell phones. No one in sight but the Russian, a pale guy with black hair, whose fanatic devotion rendered him practically fatless, everything hard about him. He bent over the water fountain, sipping a mouthful, swallowing it, sipping. If we'd exchanged more than five words within the last year, I would have asked him to spot me. But we hadn't talked since the night he walked by Laura, Joan, and me at Chi-Chi's, where he must have figured out the three of us were related. I suspected it had something to do with Joan; there were plenty here who wouldn't talk to us anymore—maybe they were realtors, contractors, building inspectors, plumbers, whatever. Maybe they thought she was a troublemaker. So went life in our town. None of that crap made any sense to me.

I lay back on the bench, still shaking in some deep basement of the self. I thought of the starkness of Joan's room, the lamp on top of the washing machine, extension cords snaking along the floor. It wasn't right that she was living like that. I kept telling her she deserved better. She deserved the second bedroom, but she wouldn't have it, wouldn't even hear of it. She claimed she liked the room just as it was. She was with us temporarily, only until she could get herself back on her feet. It was time to kick her out, she'd insisted, once she started sanding the floor, rubbing herself into its surfaces.

I lay back again. This time the bar struck me as heavier, much heavier, though certainly within the bounds of another ten reps. If I opened my mind, if I thought of it as a glass stage absolutely open to everything around me, I knew I could harness the energy in the atmosphere, the elements. I knew there was enough energy in the pea on last night's dinner plate to explode my limits. I lifted the bar. And there was Joan's low, throaty voice: preposterous, embarrassing, and marvelous all at once. Just the thought of speaking to the dead, even if it was only speaking to the air, spit into everything that was my life. I pushed back against the roar, against doubt, stupidity, the stubbornness, you name it—anything that wanted to do me in. Ten more reps. And another for good measure. The muscles in my arms saturated and burned. The pain shredded away, as if it had left me for someone else.

The Russian stepped to the water fountain, back curled as if he were protecting it from a blow. He bent over the faucet, made clean, sipping sounds like a sparrow. Then a peculiar temptation seized me: the desire to speak. Certainly not anything profound or remotely intimate, just . . . *the sky tonight: isn't it beautiful?* To let him know that I hadn't been undone by his silence, his steady work to shut me out. When I thought of the shock on his superior face!

And maybe we'd actually carry on a conversation like decent men.

I laughed louder than I'd expected, a soft bark that burred the base of my throat. I put on another forty-five for the hell of it. Oh, the weight this time: I was a column, fluted and bleached, holding up the great marbles of the Parthenon. Or better yet, the belly of heaven itself: all the souls born, died, and yet to come. But they weren't flying around up there; I refused that. None of that ever made any sense to me. If they were anywhere, they were below us, dark and dry, stacked up side by side, like glowing rods. If there was anything like a Heaven, it was somewhere in the center of the earth, in a moist, vast envelope.

But an afterlife? Really. Every time I thought about such matters I felt insubstantial, dandelion fuzz knocked about by the wind. It wasn't that I didn't think about God. It just seemed self-defeating to put too much investment into something that seemed beyond, incomprehensible, infinitely larger than myself. Wouldn't the world be in better shape if people ignored what was on the other side? As for me, every time I looked up at the sky, it brought me more trouble than not. I tried to think about hope, and my deep, deep desire to bless life, to love every living thing from apple branch to pigeon, but the harder I tried, I couldn't push through the sludge in my head. All the while a piece of me shriveled like a freeze-burned plant, as if I sensed that my uglier thoughts were heard, if not by God, then by the soil underneath my shoes, and I was already paying in ways I couldn't yet see.

The bar pressed deeper into my clavicle. It resisted all my efforts to push it skyward.

The Russian was gone. No one in that part of the gym, not even the guy with the handlebar mustache, who wiped down the machines, buzzing from bench to bench like some tanned, muscular bee. Even if I humbled myself to yell out for help, I wouldn't have been heard.

If I was lucky, I'd only come away with a band of bruises on my chest. If I was less so, I'd spend the night in the hospital with a dislocated shoulder.

The sleek white blades of the fan turned on the ceiling above, a good six inches toward the windows. Its rotation calmed me, cooling the sweat on my brows. I stared at them with such fixation that I saw a face. The face of God? I almost laughed at the grandiosity of it, in spite of my pain. It was something less expected than that, though: a woman's face. And before I named the eyes, nose, and mouth, I knew it was Joan seeing me through, Joan pulling me up the side of a building, away from the fuel leaking inside, away from the windows blowing out, one after the next. I pushed the bar as if it weighed twenty-five, not two hundred twenty-five pounds, and lay there, spent, absolutely motionless, as the Russian walked back into the room, stepped to the water fountain for another brisk sip.

"Thanks for the help, big fuck," I said to myself.

But the buds of his iPod saved me this time.

I stood before the urinal in the locker room. I sprayed an especially deep stream of yellow against the moth cake. Two guys wandered in from the pool, stepped one leg at a time out of their royal blue bathing suits, squeezed them out at the sink. Neither would have guessed the extremity of my position but five minutes before, and there was no reason to tell them that, in spite of winning, I'd died a little death. The air smelled fetid, humid, of crusty towels and bacteria. I tasted iron in my mouth. I stepped out of my pants, certain I should have felt overjoyed at my good fortune, but I only sat on the bench. I stared at the grout lines in the floor tile until I recovered myself.

I wanted to clean them with a brush until they were white as teeth.

•

If there was a difference between how Joan and I looked at things, it was something like this: think of the difference between sitting on a train backward and sitting on a train forward. If you were sitting backward, by the time your eye caught on something, say, the honey locust by the fire tower, it was already in your past; it was already sucking away from you, never to be recovered. I preferred to see what was ahead. Unlike Joan, I wanted to see my future coming toward me.

•

I still had an hour. A whole container of an hour to use exactly how I wanted. It might have been the gift of a year, handed over to me from my Russian ancestors, wrapped like a present. I drove with impressive composure to the back of the shopping center, where I parked beside a dumpster under a mimosa (messy tree: little pink wisps on my windshield) and started walking two blocks to the east, past the other houses. Something calmed me about other lives in action: the snap of green beans broken over a bowl, a downy black spaniel rolling on her back against the grass. I was shocked and silently pleased that my mouth wasn't dry, that my deodorant hadn't given out, souring my shirt, making me nasty.

"The baby's in bed," she said, upon opening the door.

"And hello to you too," I said, laughing, too happy to be stung.

She looked directly at me, flyaway pieces of blonde, waist-length hair sticking to her lips. She looked ready to taste it, the hard tang of its minerals, but she blew it away, a wicked smile on her face. That was all it took, and I pushed her backward inside her house (one step, two), nudged the door shut with my shoe, and covered her. At once I felt myself melt, a pat of butter in a frying pan. The top of my head crackled; I laughed, and I knew I was home.

How long had it been since I felt so large?

We fucked. Crude as it sounds, we fucked away the hour. There really wasn't any other word for it. We moved from the hallway, upstairs to the bed, rolling and rocking, until she was sitting on my lap, and I was pushing inside her with such force that I worried she'd bleed and think I was cruel by tomorrow. Though she seemed to be entirely into it and want it that way. She kept nodding yes and yes, and we never said a word the whole time, nothing about family or friends, or any life beyond this nine by ten-foot room with the little jalousie window overlooking the lagoon.

Her name was Janet, though I took great pains to forget her name, as I believed she did mine. We'd met six months ago, walking up and down the aisles of the Super Fresh, where she was looking for Italian breadcrumbs and I was looking for grated cheese, as it was another of those nights when Laura was working late at the store and I wanted to surprise her with pasta, a late dinner. I followed the woman to the parking lot, she slid inside her car and sat there for a moment, face turned to the left, abstractedly toward the trees. She looked ahead, challenging me, even though I couldn't quite see her features. She flashed on her headlights, then off. On and off. I did it back. Was this all that was required? God help me. Soon I was tailing the red lights of her car as it wound through the streets of Lumina.

Miraculously, we'd been able to keep things tidy, the rule being as little talk as possible, which was fine because I wasn't even sure I trusted the sound of her voice. She fucked like a woman who'd been around, which was exactly what I'd wanted. I knew she had a husband, a husband who spent a great deal of time away from home, probably with the military, a spy? There were flags flying about the house, little medals in dishes and trays, but I tried my best not to take it all in, as I was afraid we might get ourselves into trouble if we started talking. All that mattered was that she had a body completely different from my wife's. (The tight and shallow navel, the lightest blonde hair on her calves, her downy underarms.) We'd figured out a way to do what we'd needed to do without being entered by our history, the world, and that was no small thing.

I looked on the sheets for fluids spilled but everything felt dry.

The little girl—whom I never saw and never hoped to see—slept in the next room, quiet as a mummy.

I stood. I kissed her chastely, on the top of the head, only vaguely aware that I had only five more minutes to get home. She smiled ruefully, extravagantly naked, picking at the stitches of a pillowcase. The room felt stale now and stuffed, a drawer shut up with forgotten clothes. I wanted to throw open the window, to let in the smell of the lilacs and the bay, the hose water on the leaves, but I knew it was time to get on. I was needed elsewhere.

"Sweet girl," I said, regretting it as soon as it left my mouth. Her face shadowed. I left.

CHAPTER 4

Laura's face lit up as if she were staring into an aquarium. She sat on the edge of the living room sofa with unusually straight posture, eyes so lively and intense that the color looked new.

"There you are," she said.

"Baby."

I kissed her with such brisk force that my nose knocked into her cheekbone. "Ow," I said. "I didn't mean that, *shit*."

"'Ow?' Aren't I supposed to say ow?" She jerked to the left, eyes closed. "Let's try that again." And this time we met each other on the lips, a little wetly and slow. I pulled back quicker than I meant to, then went forward again, whiskers brushing her left lash. A peck now, dry as a paper towel.

"That's better," she said, closing her eyes with a smile. "You watch that thing."

"I could do some damage," I said, beating her to it, her usual line about me.

"You could do some damage."

I hugged my backpack to my chest. My breath tasted as if I'd just brushed my teeth with baking soda.

"You're later than usual."

"I didn't get to the gym till, like, nine?"

"Busy?"

"Really busy. Out of control busy. Where are all these people coming from? They don't even know how to use the equipment."

Beyond her, the kitchen was dark: peonies in their vases, knives in the drawers. Dishes drying on a pink dish towel. Out through the window, sodium vapor orange pummeled the bayberry across the lagoon. The light literally transformed the plant, otherworldly now, a hot trashy gold. "Joan around?"

"Out for the evening."

"Thank goodness."

Laura raised both brows, but I didn't explain myself. Not that I knew what the hell I meant. The conversation went its own way: water running down a chute, over rocks, obstructions. If only I could talk with such ease when I was genuinely telling the truth. Telling the truth, I only sputtered and left spastic lapses in my sentences in some effort to find the right word. Then the word I settled on tended to be less than the one I'd hoped for, less than spectacular. Why should it be so much harder to be myself?

I sat on the ottoman across from her. "What about you? How did work go?"

"I have some news," she said. Her mouth made a whistling shape, though no sound blew through it. Two notches folded above her upper lip, like a flutist about to play.

And here my hamstrings tightened. It wasn't just the smell of stale saliva on my sideburns, dark marks leaking through my thinnest skin, or even the mash of palms, still on my shoulders, back, and brows. She'd followed me. She'd hidden behind the dumpster and followed me home from the gym, I knew it. I held out my face toward her, unguarded, contrite, waiting for the slap. Maybe that was all I ever wanted: to be hit in the face until my lights went out. *Throw something at me. I dare you.*

"I thought you should know that I went to see the doctor," she said softly. "Last week."

I sat more firmly into my seat, bewildered by the strange change in currents, the wilt of her head, so shy upon her neck. Then I fell forward in my seat, grabbed onto both of her hands and pulled her toward me.

"It's okay." She laughed, kissing the top of my head. She grabbed my hands in hers and rubbed the ripped cuticles at the base of my thumbs.

"You went by yourself? Why would you do something like that? I would have gone with you."

"I know that, love."

I tipped back into the open space behind me. I folded my arms across my chest, as if protecting myself, when all I wanted was to put her in my cocoon.

She closed her eyes and nodded. "I just know that if we did it together, if we made an elaborate production about it, I'd get all worked up the way I usually do, and I'd find a way to put it off again. Who knows, maybe the stress of it would have made me feel lousy again. So last Wednesday, I was looking at the snake plant. I started talking to the snake plant, if that makes any sense. I know, I know, a snake plant. Anyway, I saw I'd been taking up too much space in your head. In Joan's head, too. I didn't like that about myself. So I just picked up the phone"—she glanced down, with tenderness, at her hands in her lap—"and decided to go it alone." She shrugged her left shoulder and held it, as if her muscles had lost their ability to release. She might have been a figure in a painting of a dancer: shoulder frozen, left leg extended off the floor, face stumped.

"Last week? When last week? Where was I?"

"Sweetheart," she said, and shook her head all around, as if trying to rouse me. "I'm okay."

"I'm sorry," I said, tears stinging my eyes.

"Are you listening to me?" Her voice lifted, though it came from deep down, a scraped place in her throat. "I had my follow-up this morning. Mammogram, clean. HIV, clean. Pap smear, clean, every test. Everything's clean and clear."

She said it again. Then, after a pause, she said it once more. The moment opened and swelled: a paper plant dropped in water. Outside, the lagoon poised itself against the tan stain of froth on the bulkhead: neither rushing in nor running out. All was still.

We stared at each other, emptied, spent. I swiped at my eyes with my bare arm. Could life contain such happiness? I wasn't prepared for it. Everything I knew about the world told me that it was brutal to expect deliverance: it was the one true path toward bitterness. The story of our endings—the way we left the planet—did not make me hopeful. (Think of Mama falling and drowning in the lagoon.) But it was tempting to believe that the pent-up tensions of the last months—the acidic stomach, the dry scoured tongue, the waking up at 3:00 a.m.—were wasted, the anxious minutes of the spiritually poor. Here stood the possible, burgeoning like a grove of fig trees, fertilized and watered, and here I dared to defy it.

"So what did he say?" I said.

"About what?"

"You went to the doctor," I said. "You still mustn't be feeling so good."

She tugged at the seam of her pants above her knee. She wouldn't look up at me. "I'm not really," she said. "I mean, I'm not feeling all that great. But I feel a lot better than I felt a few months back. And that's something. That's something I want to hold onto right now and appreciate."

"But what did he say, Laura?"

"He said he doesn't know what could be wrong with me." Her lower lip tensed along her bottom line of teeth. "Do I have to make it any clearer?"

"Well, why not? Shouldn't he know? It's that complicated? You have tests, instruments." If I hadn't been making an effort to control myself, I'd have been waving my hands.

"We're just going to wait," she said, looking off to the window frame.

"*Laura.*"

"We're just going to wait, okay? And if I don't have all my energy back, and if I still wake up with that stupid cough in the morning, then we're just going to go through another round of tests. In a few months. After the holidays."

The air outside churned with a sound like wake, but when had the boat gone by? "I don't know about this," I said, leaning backward.

"Let's not think like that right now. Think like that and we're going to make the worst thing happen. Do you know what I mean?" She smiled a warm, generous, powerful smile. "We got good news today. Let's treat it like that, all right?" She smoothed out the sofa cushion beside her, summoning me over.

I leaned into her. She leaned into me. We sat like that, our bare arms trading heat, until we didn't know whether we could stand it anymore.

"I have news myself," I said into the side of her neck, the thick vale of her hair, which smelled of grapefruit and smoke. I blew a cooling stream of air down her bare back just to see her wiggle and twist. Which she pretended to hate, but couldn't get enough of. Our little game. The joy, the joy of it.

"Stop it!" she cried.

And when I told her about the job, her eyes brightened like eyes that had been dosed with clearing drops, pupils dilating. The hazel tended toward green. And I was fourteen again, in the presence of someone certain she'd stand in the approving rain of light, on concert stages, and know without a doubt that she was wanted, necessary. How not to feel thankful in her presence, her steady, guttering flame?

"So we have two reasons to celebrate," she said, with loveliness, and walked to the kitchen. She lifted a wineglass to her bottom lip, drew in through her nostrils, and handed another to me. We stood; our glasses chinked; the clocks resumed.

She stood in front of me, glittering, beautiful. Usually at this hour, she was still so caught up in the fracas of the day (Madison, the stalled traffic on the parkway) that she'd already closed herself down minutes before she'd walked up the gravel. The last thing she needed was to put on a good face, to attend to my reports of Joan's comings and goings, the latest house down the block reduced to foundation. She simply needed to gather the house around herself, and to head down the hall to her study. In response, I'd perfected a keen detachment. I certainly knew what it was like to defend the space between our bodies on the bed some nights, for hadn't she taught me that some separation should be protected? But that wasn't the Laura I was seeing before me right now. She was all essence: an x-ray of herself. She looked directly at me, into me, as if she were seeing all my disappointments, all the times I'd failed her, and my ideals. And still she said yes to it. With two fingers, she touched my dick, my lips, my nipples, the tips of my ears. I shivered. She smiled, tentative now, tears in her eyes.

Wasn't it always easier to tussle with someone who didn't know the whole of you?

I thought of Janet walking down the hall, checking in on the little mummy, who was sleeping on her side.

"You want to fuck," I said, raising my jaw, giving her that face, that face she called my sexy face.

She sat on my lap now, hair falling into mine, setting my eyelids to flutter. "You bet."

"Well, you're on your own."

"Oh yeah?" she said, and started dashing her fists, soft, into my side, in pantomime of a fight. "Then I'm going out."

"Is that right?"

"I'm going to find a fellow who knows how to fuck."

She walked into the bedroom. Within seconds, I heard the swipe/
sweep of matches against a matchbook. I stood before the medicine
cabinet mirror, rinsing out my mouth with my maroon cup. How had
I grown into the man before me, a man who wasn't a boy anymore, but
looked like he had some years on him? Who had a stain on his canine,
though he kept putting off getting it fixed by the dentist. Who had the
thinnest layer of the unnecessary on top of his muscles, no matter how
many sets he could press. If I'd seen him shaving before the locker room
mirror, I'd think of him as a fine-looking man, a little worn out around
the edges: rough but probably a good enough fellow, in need of a hair-
cut. Still, he wasn't the me I knew from inside. The guy in the mirror
would never be a boy again, whereas I still had my whole life ahead of
me, my life of million-dollar fucks.

A brutal thought entered my imagination: if only I could unhook
myself, I'd be able to fly.

Laura lay in bed, naked now. There were dozens of candles in the
room: the ceiling above flickered as if an aquarium were suspended
above us, each fish looking down, inquisitive. I knelt above her, and
gave her my weight. I looked down into her face—the shadowed eyes,
curious and secretive, and she urged up to kiss me.

I am happy, I said over and over to myself. *I'm a lucky man.*

Her gaze called on me to look back at it, to hold it with my own, no
blinking or burrowing into myself. Usually she closed her eyes when we
made love. A certain measure of strain about it, a concentration, as if
it were duty itself, like cleaning up a room. But how much different it
was to be wholly wanted and recognized. It called me to be something,
though what would I be for her? Love. What did it mean to be love?

My wife is alive! My wife!

Then I was stuck on that bench in the gym, the bar pinning me to my
chest until I couldn't take a breath again.

I looked past her, down the hall, to a tin sconce on the wall in the
shape of a sun. Why remote to me now: the thing I could always count

on, reliable as blood? I could take two steps toward it, and I'd be back where I was standing. Two steps back: you get the idea. So something *was* wrong inside my head, my soul. It clipped me at my root; it struck me where I lived, and I couldn't for the life of me figure out why and what to do. And I'd never build my palace.

Laura said, "Someone's mind is far, far away."

"Darling?"

"You've gone away from me," she said, more patient this time. She said it in her lost, musical way, as if she knew exactly what I felt, that distance and aloneness.

"I'm right here, babe. You know that."

"If I didn't know any better I'd say you were out giving orgasms to half this town tonight."

My eyes closed. I laughed through my nostrils, grinning away with my mouth closed. *Hit me, please.* "Absolutely right—"

"I know your type," she said, finally.

"You do," I said firmly, not as a question.

"I do," she said, nodding fast. She grinned her wicked grin, butting her forehead into my own until it pressed the lights out of my eyes. "That's why I married you."

She rolled me over on my side, and I went with it, all willing, no rudder in me. Why not? She reached over my chest with her left arm, something she hadn't done in years. I reached back. And the fact that she'd put on her denim shirt, and the fact that I still had on my jockey shorts and black socks—good God. I looked down on us from those flickers on the ceiling. The picture of the two of us slapped me with light, and I'd never been anywhere but in this room, with her flesh so supple and kind and marvelously new.

My wife is alive!

CHAPTER 5

The house had been dead for years. No pants lifted off its hangers, no shirts churning in the washer. I walked through the thick, sweet, mildewed air, room to closed-up room, looking for trouble: jimmied slider handle, humming fusebox, overturned bureau drawer. But who was anyone kidding? The house could have used an intruder, someone who cared enough to covet the stuff in these junked-up rooms, the cracked slab of the jalousie porch. At its best, the house was a glorified storage locker: boxes of sheet music (*Finian's Rainbow*, *Oliver*) sat beside pitted tools, engineering books stored in apple crates. At its worst it was a mausoleum in which nothing had breathed for years. The floors almost seemed to exhale with each cautious step of mine.

I splayed my hand on the piano, played octaves up and down the scale. In terrible tune, but I liked the way it shuddered in the damp drab cave, dissonance buzzing the legs of the chairs, the hat tins filled with buttons, safety pins. Happiness had been here once. I didn't know how I knew that, but I had the sense that if I sat here long enough and played in my limited, clunky way (I could hear Laura telling me to stop the noise, please stop the noise!) I believed I'd see the children who lived here. I imagined an awkward boy playing *Where Is Love?*, while his brothers screamed outside, poured a box of laundry soap into an inflatable pool, frothing up the surface like a dessert. Wasn't that me out there with them? And the mother with her hands on her hips crying, *you'll get a rash from that water. Stay out.*

I pulled back the draperies from the window. Weeds as high as my waist, and a wooden raft pulled out of the lagoon, boards crumbling like stale wedding cake wrapped in a napkin.

Had someone died? Had the children grown up, grown distant from their parents, and spread out all over the country, made lives of their own? Had a brother fought another brother? An argument with the neighbors? Perhaps the answers could be assumed from the basket-weave fence, now greened, warped, and pocked with mildew, clearly thrown up in spite. The question was crucial: why would someone leave a house, a summerhouse, place of pleasure and rest, in this condition? Joan would have her theory: money. Little houses like these got three-quarter million dollars these days, I knew that. But that explanation didn't sit well with me. The reason people hold on to things is more complicated than that, more heartbroken and extreme. Maybe it was just a case of stubbornness, someone unable to let go, if not of a place then of a time, and they'd cling and they'd cling until death and the law did what they did to settle things.

At least someone was concerned enough to think that the house needed a friendly hand, even if it was only a single day of the week.

I leafed through the contents of a wine box. Beneath the receipts, deposit slips, news clippings, programs, and movie ticket stubs: loose snapshots of a family. A boy in bow tie and blazer, bending over a cello as if he's protecting something cherished: a brash living thing. A second boy with the pensive expression of a medieval rabbi, already mourning his lost youth, though he couldn't be a day past thirteen. They weren't the happiest children I'd ever seen, but they weren't the most desolate either. So what if they let a little seriousness drag down the corners of their eyes when they smiled? At least they weren't like my own relatives, people who tried so hard to look happy and strong
that they ceased to be human.

Well, I'd do it for them, the boys in the photographs. I picked up a cloth and started cleaning. People had no idea how fast things wanted to fall apart if left to what waited for them: rust, mold, rot, tarnish, corrosion. If only they knew, they'd be different about life, I swear it. Those boys—*men* now—would come running, from wherever city or star. They'd find out one thing: the world was never so easy to leave, however sorry your fortune.

I started in the kitchen. I powdered the countertop with cleanser; I smeared a jewel of paste wax on a paper towel. As soon as I got to working, the air in the house started moving in circles, as if the inside of it were one big sluggish soup that needed to be stirred. It didn't take long for each and every object to become closer to itself again, to gleam with the memory of its making. This kettle. It shone all the more for having been dirtied, neglected. If one of those boys ever held it again, he'd recall where he stood when his mother took it to the register, why he liked the way his fingers fit beneath the handle. He never once scalded himself on the spout, and that was what was good about it. His past, and thus his life, would become more real, if only for a passing instant, and everything around him would *lift*.

I moved from kitchen to the living room, where I started on the baseboards. It didn't take long before my mind opened up. I wasn't the tense, overly careful person that I feared I was, but someone generous and loose, capable of big ideas. I saw paintings I never could have painted if you put a brush in my hand. Brilliant slashes and swatches, triangles thick with feeling. I loved them all the more because they were private, only mine to see. The second I held them too long in my attention, however, they shook down, sprinkling like figures on a computer screen, but that was the price of the mind and the soul—do I call it the gift? And through it all, my lungs and my beating heart, so I was more of a body than when I lay back to do a bench press in the gym.

I walked back down the hall: throat sore, nose running. The sky blued beyond the stark black pine out the window. I still had three houses to check before evening!

"Thank you for cleaning up," she said.

I felt nothing like fear. Or even surprise. I looked up. The room looked brighter now, more alive, lines sharper, surfaces cleaner. Even as it dulled, emptied like tide from a cove.

"Always so skittish," she said, laughing gently. "Always convinced you weren't my sort. What did I do to deserve that?"

She held herself forward for me. The flourish of the nose, tip curved like the bell of a wind instrument. The complex color of the eye. Hazel-green, with dark orange specks. Or tan.

"Do you know me now?"

My tongue tasting of, what, ashes? Iron? Burnt. My tongue tasted of something burnt.

Mama?

•

How many years since I sat on the bed of our rental cottage, waiting for Mama to show up?

I'd been fumbling through the balled up socks in the dresser drawers. And that face in the mirror: the threaded eyes, the profusion of pores, as graceful as a teenager's. What if she couldn't stand the look of me? Or my table manners, my brawny arms: the fucking gorilla of me. I prided myself on my ability to charm the hard ones: always I had them eating from my hand. Minutes after they met me: rolling over to play dead, as if they couldn't wait to give up themselves. Not that that was my pride. I never wanted to be king. And yet? *Thirty-two years old and your life is going to be the same from here on out.* I tried to crack a smile. There was something almost edifying about tearing myself down like that.

Down the hall, the shower water banged against the scrubbed grout.

The doorbell rang. Of course it would happen now that Laura was in the shower. You think she'd have gotten ready an hour ago. Of course she'd been as accident-prone as I was: hadn't she already knocked a lampshade off the reading lamp? But that didn't mean we couldn't break and share the burden of it.

No more noise from the shower stall. "Could you get it, dear?"

I lifted my arms, urging a little groan from the belly. I thought of all those occasions in which she thought my fears were more trivial than her troubles, which were always noble, a little saintly, of a higher order. After all, she was the one who'd spent the last two years insisting that her mother was difficult. There were good reasons why we hadn't yet met, there were, although I couldn't name them just now.

Oh, I was being the asshole of my life.

"Isidore?" Laura called, a little louder.

Time slowed, and slowed some more, a lazy, yawning jaw. Beyond the window, a bicyclist skidded into our lamp post. Well, close enough. He stood astride the mugo pine, pondering the S-shape he'd engraved in our gravel.

"Mrs. Pompoleo," I said, extending my hand.

It took me a second or two to take her all in: so large was the story of her. I'd seen the pictures: You only needed to look at Laura and Joan to expect glory. But those days were behind her. Her silver-blonde thatch of hair; her eyes unfocused, and off to the side, as if she needed bifocals. I hadn't expected to see an old lady. Well, she wasn't yet an old lady, but she had the spirit of someone who'd seen enough, thank you, and was ready to go on to the next thing. (Her little shoulders, her disappointed mouth.) I looked at her face, trying to find the beautiful woman still there, but where was she now? Rather than make concessions, she'd chosen to hold onto what she'd been, no makeup, no colored hair, as if there were something heroic in that response.

"I'd feel more comfortable if you called me Mama."

She gave me a stiff hug before stepping backward, in relief. Practical, pleasant smells came off her skin: vaporizer, toothpaste, Vaseline Intensive Care.

"I'll do that, Mama." And I led her through the door.

My fears left me once we started talking. She was eager to make contact, and I was eager to please: my greatest virtue, my greatest flaw. I told her something about the gym (I made my living as a private trainer in those days); she noted the rash of mosquitoes that year. I told her about the DDT trucks I used to bike behind as a kid. She asked about the new twenty-four-hour Acme in Beach Haven Park. Had we been there yet? It wasn't aggression; her mind simply moved more quickly than mine. She was rolling toward the lights, challenging me to keep things giddy.

Then Laura stood behind the lounge chair: a towel around her head, a towel around her middle. Her smile stretched so wide that it carved new lines around her mouth. My back tightened with the wish to rush and protect her.

Who would Laura be when she was her mother's age?

"Hi, Mama," Laura said.

"You're not dressed yet?"

No resentments, no little guilts. Their banter sounded as if they'd been walking in and out through each other's kitchens since the dawn of time. The underlying desire for routine seemed to quiet their misgivings. I had the sense that the largest problems were being put to rest for now. And I was grateful to stand outside their circle of light, to watch like a guest.

"I'm running a little late," Laura said.

"You finish getting dressed" Mama said. "I'll hug you in a minute, dear."

"I'll be right back." Laura adjusted the towel on her head, ignoring the signals on my face. "I'm glad the two of you are getting to know each other."

I hitched my palms into my underarms. The back of my shirt was already drenched as if I'd showered in it. Apple cores. Where was this smell of rotting apple cores coming from? You guessed.

"He's a good guy, isn't he?" Laura said.

Mama folded her hands delicately on her lap.

"Anything I can do to help?" I said, calling over my shoulder.

But she'd already left the room. Talk, talk, chatter, rasp. Talk, talk, chatter, rasp. I've had all kinds of work in my life—ditch digger, short order cook on the boardwalk—but no work as stressful as carrying on a conversation with Mama—I'm serious. How long was it—ten minutes, twelve? I pictured my eagerness to please as a living thing, with brittle legs: stupid and shiny as a wood tick. It crawled outside the room toward a dog, a human ankle, a creature to feast on. It wanted to be fat with it, to swell with blood. Then I never wanted to see that sorry tick face ever again.

Her mouth kept moving like a movie of a mouth. There had to be something out there, inside me, to focus her attention.

And here's what the insiders knew, what they always knew, and didn't want you to find out: language was an animal. Neglect it, forget to tend it and feed it well, and there it was, knocking you down with its big wet paw, breathing its toothy breath in your face. And what did you have to defend yourself, but a loneliness so stark that you couldn't even feel its workings in you?

Then Laura walked into the room, hair dried, combed, brushed, every last curl tamed and conditioned. She perched on the arm of my chair, placed her hand on top of my head, claiming me. She did it with such ready assurance that I instantly leaned into her just-bathed fragrance. I felt so loved (and loving) that it didn't matter to me how the rest of our lives would turn out.

"You're a lucky girl," Mama said, smiling up at her daughter. Mama reached for my hand. A lightness, a rising up in me, like going over the top of a Ferris wheel. Who would have thought?

Laura said, "And he's lucky too."

Hand squeezed hand squeezed pretty slender hand. Somewhere birds, out of earshot, sang in agreement.

•

But my relationship with Mama never advanced beyond the polite. Not that we ever had a flat-out argument; we never breached that kind of intimacy. I simply made it my duty to make sure I was fixing the truck or scrubbing the bathroom if I knew she was coming to stay for a few hours. I believed it was better for us to spend as little time with one another in the same room, and I think she agreed. I'd bet every last dollar in my sorry checking account that she'd actually decided, months before me met, that we'd never be close. I wasn't exactly what she'd hoped for in a son-in-law.

Maybe she simply sensed that women hadn't raised me. My own mother had died in a car accident, long before I was old enough to mourn the weight of her hand upon my head. Could Mama have sensed that about me? I grew up in a house of men: my father, my uncle Moishe, my cousin Danny. We lived in our own protected bubble for years, making it up as we went along, indifferent to the customs of the outside world. Ignorant. We never ate dinners around the table like the families of my friends; we didn't say prayers. Instead, we slurped scalding pizza off paper plates in front of the evening news. We ate stews, steaks, baked potatoes—heavy foods that filled and nourished us and made us feel solid. In the center of the living room stood a barber's chair, on which various members of the household took turns cutting each other's hair. But the house wasn't a shambles. Anything but. As a matter of fact, it was one of the loveliest in Aberdeen, with its expertly trimmed privet, its grand flowerbeds: hollyhock, foxglove, poppy, zebra grass, lace cap hydrangea, oak leaf hydrangea. Three years in a row we won the Strathmore Home Improvement Competition. And yet our rituals would have shocked the families of my classmates. When did you last go into a household where you were expected to lift the toilet seat on leaving the bathroom? I'd thought that that was common until Sherri Blatt, my first girlfriend, admonished me for such carelessness in her house. How could I not feel bewildered and ashamed for not knowing the most obvious thing?

Given my upbringing, it made sense that I'd find myself, as a grown man, in a house of women. Wasn't that always the way? They made life seem exceptional after all those years of the dour: the thick smells, the curds of shaving cream with their sharp black whiskers. I loved their voices chiming through the glassware in the rooms, I loved their smells: laundry soap, herbal tea, patchouli, lavender. They couldn't have been further from the men of my upbringing with their thick, brandied moods, their eyes trained on the sports and financial pages. These women revitalized my life for me. They took me to another place, a planet with perfumed trees that dusted the air every time the wind blew through them.

But that didn't mean I ever felt quite at home here.

CHAPTER 6

Sunday night, 9:45. The garbage put out at the curb, the broiled chicken wrapped in foil. Children bathed, read to, put to bed. People in front of the computer, or with the newspaper, as if the longest night in history lay in wait.

If time could be sweetness, this was it. Sunday night, the sweetest night of the week.

And lonesome too, slightly blue. All that work about to begin again, grinding and dull, on the other side of sleep. A hell denied.

All the while Joan got a leg up on them. I stood outside her closed door, as tapping, crisp and percussive, filled the hall. I'd never heard such breakneck typing. I imagined it as the sound of someone trying to keep herself awake through the nights and days.

I knocked softly, then twice more, louder. I gripped the address book in my hand, certain now that she'd see through my ruse to speak with her.

"It's open," Joan said, friendlier, more worn down than I'd expected.

"This was out on the kitchen table. I didn't want it to end up in the wrong pile and get thrown out."

Joan sat at her folding table, spine straight, hair falling down her back so that the light caught its reddish-gold streaks. She looked at the screen. I placed the address book beside her, stepped backward. Now that I was inside, I felt the walls cramming. Somehow it seemed wrong that I wasn't back outside, sweeping the pods and dead leaves off the deck. Once I made up my mind to do something, it was crucial I finish, as if the well-being of my lost ancestors depended on it.

"Oh, thanks." She glanced up, met me eye to eye, and took in the cartoon of the big red bull on my shirt, as if it seemed all wrong on me. "What are you up to?"

"Looks like you're working."

"Trying. I'm not sure if that counts." She shook her head, closed down her document with a ding.

I eased myself down on the mattress and looked about. The place looked small, even smaller than the last time I'd seen it: a five by nine cell, with white walls, folding table, lamp, and a mattress atop red plastic milk crates. Above her desk, she'd tacked up a clipping of a man standing face to face with a deer. She deserved better. This was not what we wanted for her, and I hated seeing her wishes played out. But I'd have given anything to have such a place of my own. The truth was, Laura and I had moved into Mama's house with haste. My tools, sat, next to her sewing kit, my dumbbells next to her Dusty Springfield records, so that our worlds were mixed up, disorderly, a salad of confusion.

"I'll be doing this kind of thing when I'm an old broad." She scrolled, scribbled some notes, scrolled, scribbled again. The writing on her notepad was so personal, so full of backward slants and scrolls that I wondered whether she'd been crazy all along and I hadn't taken in it. But how fascinating the motion of her hand! She gripped her pencil not with her forefinger, but between the thumb and the middle. "Richard's asked me to do some research on ospreys."

"Oh, Richard." I gave his name all the graceful weight of a cinderblock.

She looked at me with half-parted mouth. "That doesn't sound like you."

"Oh, you know. If only we could all be so good at doling out the work and taking the credit for it." I attempted a smile.

"Really?"

I shifted from side to side, folding one leg on top of the other, even though it hurt my back. I suppose I was trying to see how far I could go. I never liked running people down, especially to those who thought well of them. But Richard? Richard was clearly out for himself, even if he'd presented himself as someone of compassion and principle. Sure, he'd done a lot of good by helping to organize the townhouse protest, but he'd done a lot of bad too, especially on the personal level, pitting one neighbor against the next and so on. And I never liked the way he'd treated Joan. He took clear advantage of her need to have a purpose at a time when she was feeling down, way down, and had good reason to feel like that. And did he manage to make her feel that her contributions were worthy? I mean, here was a woman who went door-to-door, soliciting signatures. I couldn't think of anything as stressful or as thankless. She was often treated like shit; once someone even threw her own pen at her, and you could see what it did on her face some nights. The tiredness. There were never enough signatures, just as there was never enough enthusiasm, belief, or fight in her. And Amy, his assistant? Well, she did her part to make sure Joan was always a step out of the loop. And she liked to isolate her in public ways; I'm talking planning board meetings, the zoning board. Holding a conversation with Richard in Joan's presence while pretending Joan wasn't standing right there.

I mean, we were talking about the director of the high school marching band here!

Joan directed a rueful look toward the side of her screen, as if hearing such things made her heart speed. Then she let out a laugh from way down deep, thick with frustration. "Well, if it wasn't for Richard I'm sure this town would have been handed to the builders ages ago."

But Mama's house would also be worth twice what it is today. Though I'd be half-cracked to say such a thing aloud.

51

She went back to her keyboard. I felt as low as they came: she knew how to make you feel you deserved that when it was warranted. And yet the top of my scalp tingled as if it had been rubbed down with alcohol. I wanted to shout. I wanted to hoot out everything I'd been afraid to speak. It felt wonderful, like chewing on gemstones. For God's sake, you might have thought I'd insulted Jesus Christ himself, which was enough to make me want to tear down some statue, cart it away in pieces. How could anyone's devotion be that encompassing?

And what of Mama's face in my imagination, that voice coming at me in that strange and sad house? It was here again, taunting me. I shut my eyes. And still it was there, glittering, pious.

"Are you all right?" Joan said, blinking.

I looked down at the salt stains on my work boots. I hardened my expression, brushed off the cuffs of my pants. *Face, go away.*

"Liar," she said, wounded, with a little scorn.

"Who's lying?"

"Why are you sitting like that?"

I looked down at myself. Who knew that I hadn't given my full weight to the mattress? My ass hung halfway off the edge.

"Move back now, relax."

Joan sat beside me. I felt as I felt when she first moved in, and I couldn't figure out how to arrange my eyes and arms whenever she talked to me. I fought back the urge to stand up and walk.

Joan moved closer. I saw my soul up and leave me, a bird go up in the highest tree, where it wouldn't be hurt, and it wouldn't hurt back. If she knew what was good for her, she'd have stayed exactly where she was, keeping free space between us. As it was, the power in that opening felt so strong I imagined it setting off car alarms, metal detectors, gauges of every size and sort. Not that I had any intention of touching her, by God. But how could I resist such buzzing, frenetic energy? Once I touched someone, and I was touched back, it was as if my hands started working with a life of their own, nurturing and greedy. And I

52

couldn't let that happen now. Too much had gone down over the years, too many women, so many beautiful, squandered hours, and I longed for another life, a life of decency and use.

If only she knew how she looked when the lamplight hit her face. I swear she'd be a different person, calmer, with less to prove.

"So tell me about ospreys," I said.

"Ospreys are mysterious. Ospreys are alive. Ospreys have six-foot wingspans. Ospreys mate for life."

Then the parade of gorgeous facts. How I loved hearing about her love for things.

In a while things turned easy and relaxed. As long as we focused on ospreys, not on love or power or the plottings of the builders, we were able to stand inside ourselves, and we could be, for each other, the sister (or brother) each of us had wanted but never had.

"Are *you* okay?" I said, and placed my hand on her arm.

Joan was in a funny position, her neck crammed up against the wall, so that she had to turn her head leftward in order to fit. How could she not have been thinking about Mama, the subject so large that we were afraid to touch it, lest it pull us down the suckhole?

"Thank you," she whispered. As if the question itself meant more than the answer.

"Are you comfortable like that?"

She nodded. She rested the back of her head on her folded arm. I tried to give her more pillow, but she waved me away. We didn't say anything for the longest time. We didn't need to: outside, the swallows in the slash pines seemed to talk for us, give us all the sounds that we needed. She outlined shapes with her fingertip, curious shapes bowed with lines and harsh, flamboyant dashes. It was tempting to ask her what she was drawing, but that would have stopped her, would have clamped down her imagination. Better, finally, to ride inside those impulses. I went to palaces on mountaintops, nests made of dried grass, feathers, paper, mud, rubber bands.

The light changed in the room, first blue, then bluer, then the barest white light as her laptop ticked off.

How long had Laura been standing there? It seemed preposterous that Joan and I hadn't heard her footsteps, or the drop of her coat upon a chair, but she stood a bit back from the doorway now, with an expression both relieved and parental. Too cautious to step forward. Though her skin had its usual glow, her hair looked heavy, as if exertion were dulling its shine. Seconds passed before Joan and I curled away from each other. Still, we lay there, rested and refreshed.

"Come on in, you," Joan said. "Sit down with us. Put up your feet. We're having a party. A pajama party."

Laura behaved like someone new to the street, a woman who had wandered through the open door, asking after her lost cat.

"Laura," Joan said, laughing, raising her palm up and down. "It's *us*."

"I'm starved," Laura answered. "I need something to eat."

Joan smoothed the patterns on the bedspread. "I'll get it. What would you like, a sandwich, some soup?" She was already halfway down the hall before she finished her sentence.

"How did it go today?" I propped myself up by my elbows, surprised by how calmly, sanely I presented myself.

"Soup," Laura said, projecting her voice. "Gazpacho. There's a container on the top shelf of the refrigerator."

I said, softly, "Sweetheart?"

"Yes?"

"Sit with me. How was the store? You must have been there pretty late."

Laura shrugged. She didn't answer. But *some*thing was on her mind. Maybe she recognized—I only saw it now—that the two of us hadn't lain together in bed, outside of sleep, in months. We'd made love of course, but beastly frenzy couldn't quite compare to lying side by side—spacious, in divine aimlessness—without an ending in mind. Whatever it was, her demeanor seemed practically relaxed now, free of resentment. Not like past incidents when her reaction ran hushed and deep and chilled. Her shrug seemed to express the weight of a trying day, even though I swear, for just a second, her eyes filled.

If anything, she looked mysteriously—can I say it now, from the other side?—hopeful? kind?

For some reason it came to me that I was losing her.

I reached for her hand, which she let me hold. "Well, you look great," I said.

"Thank you," she said, looking everywhere at the room but at me. "You do too."

"I mean it," I said. And I did.

●

I lay in bed late at night, sweat filming my upper lip. The view outside the window was entirely black, no hint of dawn. I'd already pushed down the covers on my side. Laura turned toward me, her mouth parted, breath still minty with toothpaste. Even when it was hot in the room, her hands and feet were perennially cold, so she pushed into the heat of my chest and legs. Somewhere, out over the bay, a boat horn groaned into the night. The atmosphere felt sluggish and thick, no manufactured wind streaming from the vents. I stared at the fullness of Laura's lips, the dense fall of her hair framing her cheeks, but the dark obscured her features. I almost reached for her face: *My heart. You're the last one I'd want to hurt.*

I dug around with my feet for her hot water bottle. Sure enough, it lay inches from her ankles, tepid now, as awful as an organ that had fallen from her body. I rolled out of bed, lugged it to the bathroom to fill it again. The faucet sparkled. The dark drain chugged. The bottle gulped with almost human intention: insatiable, swelling, the deep red-pink of candy. Lurid now. Monstrous. And intimate.

Was it ever possible to love two people, wholly, equally, at once?

●

Joan couldn't see me from where I parked: the foliage too thick, the early spring leaves as wide as shovels. But what pleasure it was to hold her in my gaze without feeling awkward or ashamed, even if she was a good two hundred feet away. (Was it time I started thinking about glasses? The movements of her face were all but indistinguishable from my place in the driver's seat.) Enough, though, to know that she had a life and a purpose away from the domain of our house. She thrived here, clearly; she didn't need us, and the thought that she'd be gone before the end of the year made my eyes hurt. She stood outside a freshly shingled house with a woman. Strict white permanent, tan Hush Puppies—so this was Hazel Luce, the builder's advocate. Joan appeared to direct all her energies into calming herself, for I'd never seen her carry a conversation without turning her head or moving her arms and hands for expressive effect. Those arms lay motionless against her side now, practically pinned, which told me everything I needed to know about Hazel, who faced Joan with chin raised and arms braced across her chest. How close Hazel was to stomping her left foot, kicking Joan in the ankle! But Joan didn't know it. Sometimes you needed a little distance in order to see clearly.

●

Inside the window of her store, Laura stood with her back against the wall. She crossed her arms. Madison sat beside her on the waxy, wooden floor. It was just after ten. The store closed for the night: the drawers counted, shipments processed and placed on shelves. I looked for the dreaming girl on the high school stage, the girl who was so much more than her classmates and teachers combined. There was a version of her standing there, but she looked depleted, a little ashen in the face, as if nothing would please her more than to rid herself of music tonight, with all its implicit hopes. As to whether life could still change: I don't think she had an answer.

56

Why didn't I go in? Why put them in a position where they'd be puzzled and shocked if they found me parked across the street, my forehead smudging the window glass? Maybe my bounding into the store would be shock enough: more dissonance than they deserved at the end of a day. Or maybe I worried that I played some small part in the making of that defeated expression: if I'd been a better, more attentive husband, I'd have at least helped to *distract*. A car approached from the train station, a strange car, impossibly slow, headlights as blue-bright as a flashbulb, a car bomb sustained. The car slowed some more, and I heard my chin drop against the wheel. Gangland: single shot through my brow. Brain shattering light, mouth leaking blood. Every crease and shadow of my clothes overlit as homemade porno. But it was only a police car, some cop on the lookout for drug dealers. I nodded to the man I couldn't see inside, glanced over my shoulder, and pulled away, with the strictest caution, into the wiped out avenue.

•

He stood half-a-head taller than Joan. He wasn't actually a boy—even from a few hundred feet away I saw the dense stubble on a jaw; he had to have been twenty-five. But there was a boyish quality to his slouch, his loping walk, his shy, goofy pleasure in being led around. They walked up driveway after driveway to tell people about the planning board meeting next week. I liked her parental, almost teacherly air: her stepping to one side to let the boy approach, her encouraging gaze, free from condescension. Her genuine smile after it was clear they'd made contact with a supporter, someone who believed that the delights of Lumina were being harvested by sharks. They laughed together; they discussed things. How welcome to see that she could be a winning leader: someone who had the confidence to divide and share her power without believing she was under threat.

•

The new house was becoming itself. Once they figured out I wasn't a henchman for the Mob, the workmen welcomed me on-site, even calling me Mirsky. I offered them coffee from my plaid thermos; they offered me good cheer, stray boxes of nails, and switches. I thought of the houses I had to check, the last of which had a living thing with a rank woody smell (a raccoon? a skunk?) inside its crawlspace. And then there was Craig Luckland's car, which I'd been promising to check out for weeks. I didn't mind looking at cars, whatever. Nothing could match the kick of joy I felt upon hearing a long-dead starter turning over with ease again. But the idea of sliding around on my back on Craig's cold and greasy garage floor while he talked about his glory days on the reality show. *Fuck off, Mr. Office of the Law.*

I studied the peaks of the house. Actually it was no longer a house. Freaking Parthenon was what I called it: it could have contained three of our house, with more space left over for a lap pool and sauna. All my life I'd lived in places too small for me: I was constantly negotiating tight spaces; I reached around others to take the kettle off the stove, to slice a piece of cheese or whip up egg whites. The mere notion of volume, the ability to hide in your own room so you could talk to yourself—it seemed heartbreakingly rich. Imagine, having a workshop to house my tools! And Laura: she wouldn't need to keep parts of her record collection in the hallway, in dusty piles, which I always needed to clean.

Of course Joan would have been ashamed to hear me voice such a wish. But I should have been allowed to dream, right?

Then rage drew its claws across my back. I was angry with myself for settling with so much less than I could have had. None of these people with fat bank accounts worked any harder than I did. I was no idiot; I'd finished college: I could have been selling real estate like Ferris, or making art, selling paintings for tens of thousands of dollars a piece. Maybe I'd simply lived with the deepest abiding certainty that all good things would come to me. If I didn't think too much about money, it would certainly rain itself on my head—at least the pleasures and comforts that money could give. And it wasn't that I'd gotten a mean deal—I mean, look at the house we were living in! But one day you woke up and realized that the choices had already been made for you. If you'd decided that you weren't at heart a rich man, the world wrote its choices on you. And you weren't in for any grand surprises. And, without even knowing it, you weren't seeing the doctor for check-ups, you weren't buying insurance, you weren't opening retirement accounts, even preparing for a future beyond the next six weeks, because it scared you to death to entertain the possibility that anything could go wrong, and you had absolutely no reserve to deal—mentally, figuratively, financially, literally.

I stopped at the store on the way to the Gitterman house. Outside the automatic doors a woman close to my age sat on the concrete and held out her palm. With the exception of a broken front tooth, she didn't look much different from the shoppers who pushed their carts past her. A broad-faced, girlish woman with tanned skin, cropped hair and thin metallic earrings in the shape of exclamation points. One after another, people walked by her with lowered heads. Maybe she'd have done better if she'd worn soiled rags or rubbed herself between her legs. Approaching her, I felt the depths of her awareness flash on me: a big bright hope that I'd give her something more than the ceremonial quarter. I reached into my wallet, drew out a dollar bill. And just as my hand touched hers, I felt her shudder through me. She placed the dollar in her front pocket with a whiff of disgust as if I'd never be able to give her what she needed.

CHAPTER 7

Hazel Luce walked in between our yard and the next, stepping around dusty millers, prickly pear, chinquapins. She lifted up a trash can lid. She squatted, sifted through a pile of mulch with open hands. She smelled her hands. Not a qualm in the world about walking on private property. (If *I* did such a thing, I'd soon be lifting broken chunks of concrete, in an orange jumpsuit, with a rifle pointed at my back.) Her face had the glassy, starved look that came from fixing too long in front of a computer screen to the exclusion of the world outside. It was the kind of look I needed to stay away from, for if I allowed myself to take it fully in, I'd: a) start to worry myself; b) be drawn into whatever she was doing, in order to feel some power over it.

And what Hazel was doing didn't involve life and death: you could tell from the way she kept pulling in on her cigarette. And I just had to finish Luckland's car, which I'd already kept longer than I needed to. I deliberately turned my back to her, because I knew she wouldn't let me go if our eyes met. That type always latches onto me, believe you me. They can smell my need to be helpful, stinky as a pheromone, and it makes them dive and buzz: the drunk and wounded bees.

No, I practically said aloud. *I will not lift a finger for you.*

I knew who she was. She knew who I was. We'd talked once, months back, at the hardware store. Something about the price of clothesline, or the inferior lighting in the aisles, but for weeks afterward we'd passed each other on the streets without a nod, always gazing straight ahead, as if the duty to recognize one another was one that needed to be fought off at any cost. So much for the myths of community life. It was the way you conducted yourself in Lumina. You couldn't say hello to everyone you passed on the street. No one had use for that kind of intimacy. So you had to set limits: *You had to say you are my friend, and you are not.* A glorified high school, but so what? I never took it personally.

Hazel had every reason to hate me, given who'd been sleeping in our laundry room, but she was probably too wrapped up in her own concerns to worry about that. If she did worry, there was something remotely satisfying about the fact that I probably counted for more in her mind, especially because I had as much political power as a tuna casserole. On the list of things that mattered to her, people, I imagined, were probably pretty far down the list. They only looked out for themselves when they were backed into a corner, so why not put your faith in something that didn't have a brain and soul capable of evils?

Her elbows were so thin and crepey that I wondered if her primary source of nutrition could have been nicotine, poor thing.

"You haven't seen a dog around here, have you?"

I wagged my head, but made sure to keep my eyes on the carburetor.

I clutched the wrench tighter. Even the thickest soul could have heard the wobble and pleading in her voice. She'd needed my help; there was no choice for me now. And I lifted my face.

"How long has he been missing?"

"Thirteen hours," she said, looking at her watch, "and forty-five minutes."

Indeed. She could have said anything else, but her answer drew me to her. It was as if a thunderhead of cooling relief had fallen on my face. Now that I'd given up, I felt that the world was in its proper order: I thought back to the day when Craig Luckland gave me my job, and how inviting it was, finally, to roll over and play dead.

We dedicated ourselves to pretending we were new to each other, as if it were too much to bear the pressures of our resentments.

But what if Joan and Richard happened to be careening down the street in his old yellow Saab, too fast, pitiless? I pictured them coming upon our conversation, their faces both passionate and curious, their feelings so strong they had a sexual current. They couldn't breathe evenly, couldn't look me in the eye. No question I betrayed them. *No*, I said, emphatically no, the contents of my stomach fizzing as if carbonated. And the last thing I wanted to do was to pit them against me, to push them closer to one another. I mean Joan knew exactly what she was doing. She was perfectly capable of taking care of herself, but anyone could see that she'd never get exactly what she needed from Richard: she'd always be outshone. And he'd hurt her one day, he would. He was just waiting for that moment when someone brighter and more eager showed up on his front step. And Joan wouldn't take to it well. She'd be stunned, crushed, as much as she liked to think she was made of thicker skin. Just look at the way she'd behaved after Mama's death, as if the simple fact of her leaving was her doing.

I couldn't take my eyes off Hazel. She couldn't take her eyes off me. Why spend the bulk of your energies standing against your neighbors? Why bind yourself to powers that would cut out your liver in your sleep once you gave them what they needed? Money, a new roof, dinners at elegant restaurants, friendships with the business elite: call me naive, but that wouldn't do it for me. Maybe all she'd ever known was hardness and rejection. Maybe she was still the high school senior who had never gotten to be class president because of what she was: a strict, unfeminine thing, who didn't have it in her to charm the boys or win over the teachers and the staff. And that fighting, that *difficulty,* had started to feel like life itself, and without it, there was only numbness, and she weighed as much as a dried-out seed pod.

When did things start shifting between us? Standing this close to her made me—what? Defensive? She seemed to see me getting nervous and she seemed to enjoy it. The corner of her mouth turned up: a smile and a smirk. Perhaps she was used to bringing that out in others, waiting for the turn. For a moment, it was hard not to despise her for her wish to set herself apart. The little narcissism of thinking she was unique and smarter than everyone else, with their sad, weak need to be liked.

"I'll ask around," I said, turning my back to her. "I'll let you know if I see him."

"Will you?" she said, as if she hadn't, until this moment, recognized who I was.

The trees above seemed to bear down into her question. Even the birds went nuts. They chattered and peeped; they screamed like sirens.

•

In an impossible world, one on the left, the other on the right. Equal pressure given and returned through our hands. Neither pulling me closer, neither pushing me away. Walking forward into the burning star of evening, unimpeded. What we did to the air! See how it stirred things up. And the people walking past us, wanting to feel us on their arms and faces.

Stop it, I said, tensing my hamstrings, the cords in my calves. *Stop it, right now.*

•

I shouldn't have done it. I knew I'd already regret it and pay, years in the future, but the shock opened me up. I felt delirious, raw, as if cells were being dragged from the inside of my cheek to be placed on a slide.

Joan and I walked through the bedroom wing of the Blatherwick house, second on my list. The rooms were so large that they were impossible to overload, even with the largest furniture. It was no secret that Jack Blatherwick was one of the principals behind New Lumina and Launch Haven. A lawyer, he played a large part in making sure that the old ranchers were being torn down and townhouses built. It certainly didn't hurt that his wife, Ivy, sat on the planning board, or that Jill Peatman, his daughter-in-law, made sure the projects of associates passed quickly, without much fuss. Somewhere, deep in the study upstairs, there were memos, letters, files. Documents that could be of use to us. Proof. Still, that fact was so large that we dared not speak it aloud. It rang through all our silences, the soles of our shoes on the floor. A cold, spacious feeling expanded in my stomach. And we weren't the kind of people to take advantage like that, we weren't.

The carpet smelled fresh, adhesive, impossibly new.

Joan walked up and down through the halls, a little quiet, but deeply interested at the same time. She picked up the occasional vase and rubbed it on her skirt, as if she thought it best not to leave a little of herself behind. It was something to see what she made of the place. She didn't rant or roll her eyes. Instead, she stepped ahead as if the rooms were a stage on which she was going to audition for a role that might prove to end her career. How was it possible that the house could be so spotless and remote, so little lived in, without nicks, tears, and spills? If life were still possible for the place, it would only happen once others had moved in, layering it with the smells of roasts and plants, the dents of heels on the floor, and so many ghosts.

Joan stopped suddenly, eyes curiously open and alert. I thought of the cold pale watery yogurt I'd eaten for breakfast that morning; it still shivered in my stomach, sickening me. "Are there security cameras in here?"

The joke of it left her face a little tired, concerned. It made sense that all this faceless stuff—the crème-colored cushions, the technological gadgets already on the way to being dated—were bought with the flat-out hope that they'd be coveted by intruders. Why else want them unless someone else wanted them? And what of the workers paid to look after your house? Didn't they too need to be watched with extra care? In the back of my brain, Uncle Moishe, dead twenty years, rubbed a yellow rag over the doorknobs of our house, just to make sure the police had a clean surface to dust for fingerprints. All the while the rest of us sat in the hot car, waiting to go to Asbury Park, to play miniature golf by the boardwalk.

"Doesn't it feel like the kind of place that would have security cameras?" Joan said, more softly, the slightest thrill punching up her voice.

"I'm sorry," I said, "that's paranoid." But just as I'd said it, I shook my head. Wasn't I in the business of the paranoid?

"Paranoid, look who's talking, paranoid."

"Now that, my dear, is getting paranoid."

"I'm serious. You really don't think they're watching us?"

I looked up to where I decided a camera might be. Joan looked up too. We stood across from each other, looking at each other look.

What if I let my heart move? What if I went for her right at that moment?

Outside the raindrops fell on the leaves with a curious sound of frying.

•

I saw the signs long before I saw the people holding them.

They clumped outside the municipal building, lining either side of the main walk. It was impossible to get to the front door without passing through their ranks. I knew their ways. I'd seen their signs outside the marina, outside the supermarket: words, brainless words that screwed themselves into your imagination, and looked to nothing beyond the gratification of the present: SEWERS FOR ALL! PIPING PLOVERS TASTE LIKE CHICKEN! The town would only get more crazed as we got closer to the night of the planning board meeting.

I parked beneath the spreading limbs of an ancient maple. The tree had thinned considerably since my last visit; feeble wet shreds weeping piece by piece onto my hood. I sat there for longer than I care to name, imagining the damage they'd do to my paint. My keys dangled from the ignition. What if I backed up right now, said *fuck, no* to my plans, and drove down the street to Janet's? Her bedroom with its closed-up, sour drawer smell; my mouth moving in her hair; the little girl in her pajamas, in deep sleep, clutching her stuffed ducklet on the opposite side of the wall. Just the possibility of fifteen minutes of rip-roaring vitality slapped me awake, bonked me with light, and now the maple tree, the grass, the browning pink rose by the bench—all of it trembled and glowed, mere seconds from igniting. But Janet had gone to Florida for the week, and I'd been putting off that talk with Craig Luckland for too long. The bastard owed me cash. Wouldn't you know that his engine left a minor constellation of stains on our driveway, which wouldn't wash off, God damn.

I walked forward, concentrating into the cedar shake shingles on the roof: the mold, the pale green threads of lichen furring up the wood. I tried to look stuporous, a little out of it, if only because I didn't want to give them what they wanted. There, the supermarket manager with the unbalanced glasses; there, a man with a clean ace bandage wrapped ten times around his arm. There, Chick Keatley; there, Betty Bridges; there, Kevin Honeysett in an expensive satin tie, pink as a rhododendron. They didn't yell or even talk among themselves. Something shuffled, something scraped. They'd become their own thing now, a single force with a single unalterable face, fatigued and defiant. *We've waited too long for what we want; we've been duped, and time's running out faster than you think.*

The adrenaline slowed me, drugging me, dragging me down. I walked forward, eyes fixed to the pavement. Venom burning with such force on the back of my neck, I thought I had a rash.

•

The gym was empty that afternoon, a dump for damp towels and water bottles. No two dumbbells of equal weight stacked side by side. I
closed in on the flat bench near the windows, slid on so many plates I'd
forgotten to count. I centered the space between my shoulder blades
on the vinyl, staring up into white astringent lights. Too much banging
inside the head: the picketers, Janet far away in some Florida wasteland,
no doubt fucking some thug in her mother's bed while she was out at
choir practice. And Craig Luckland. Why hadn't he shown up as he'd
said? Something tempting about the possibility of ruining myself: no
Russian or anyone else to help me if need be. The hot, purpled thrill of
being pinned to the bench again. Still, twenty reps were mine, all mine,
my muscles contracting, pushing up against the shit of life.

•

Laura and I knelt into the crushed rocks one cloudy afternoon, pulling
weeds. Glarey clouds ragged in from the bay. I thought of our backyard
the way I thought of my plaid hunter's jacket: you wear it over and over
for its broken-in look, the missing button on the sleeve, the threads un-
raveling at the collar, until one day you realize that it wasn't the jacket
you thought it was. Sheer use has worn it out, and you weren't even
as dashing as the homeless woman with the outstretched hand at the
supermarket.

We worked from opposite ends, sweet Laura by the lagoon, me by the
deck. I loved the rhythm of weeding: picking, tossing, picking, tossing. Our plan was to work toward the center of the yard, which we'd
marked with a croquet wicket. A game was being made of it. Laura was
clearly winning, but I was gaining on her fast, despite myself. By my
side, the rocks gleamed with an intensity that made them look nude.
They wanted their weeds back; they wanted cover. How embarrassed

they were to be seen and scorned, in all their lowly rockness! Like Joan: wasn't that something she'd say? Certainly she wasn't very far away, but she felt far away, thousands of miles away, Copenhagen, Moscow, or Sri Lanka, even as I'd just seen her that morning in our very kitchen, pouring pancake batter into a hot skillet. Burning it, of course. Filling up the room until the smoke detectors screamed. And, oh, the high spitting of the alarm. Dogs barking down the street. Smoke clouds filling up our bellies. And the three of us practically dancing about the kitchen, beating at the air with cheesecloth and wet dishtowels.

"Smells fantastic." Laura sat back on her heels, nose lifted. She expanded her chest, looked around at the yard with a calm, centered smile.

"Give me a kiss." I crawled toward her, destroying the knees of my jeans.

•

In a box, in a far back corner of a closet, there was a picture of me. I didn't know why I hadn't gotten rid of it: probably out of respect for my wife, who took the photo years back, during a passing moment when she snapped pictures of everything (cereal boxes, spoons, macramé plant holders). I'm looking straight on, the yellow wall making a corona around my close-cropped head. But that's not what bothers me. It's the fact that there are two people in that face. Use your hand, cover each half. The right side: So wolf-like and full of suffering (eyes turned down, mouth turned slightly up) you just know, whatever the guy's choices, he's hellbent toward setting himself on fire. And the other half? So purified, detached, and above it all (brow arched over an opened, rounded eye) that he's not even human. A holy man, a Byzantine monk. He's not even here.

CHAPTER 8

Okay, my man.

You're going to tell her what you've been thinking. Not a week from now, not two.

Tomorrow.

I know you want to shut me up. I know you want to stuff my throat with worn socks and kick me into the crawl space. But the wanting is killing you, until you're hardly even a man anymore. Isn't she just waiting for you to say it, to speak it aloud? And who's to say that your plan won't help her to live more fully, to defeat the project she's been trying to defeat?

It'll happen like this.

The two of you alone, at home, Laura off yet again, at the store, at a meeting of the business guild. You'll be standing at the kitchen counter, maybe cutting things up for a salad, the two of you tossing walnuts, cranberries, spinach, carmelized onions into the silver tureen.

You'll say, "I have something I want to say."

Joan will just look at you with that marvelous, blank stare.

"I want to sleep with you."

She'll let out a high nervous laugh, more cough than laugh, a response uncharacteristic of her. "Excuse me?" A little softer than you expected, a little frightened, wary. For a moment you'll be put off, for she'll hold her arms close to herself, like a suit of armor. And doesn't she have every right to be scared?

"I'm not talking about love, or a relationship. All I want to do is to touch you." And you'll say it exactly the way you feel it, no gap between your thoughts and your words. No selfishness, no brutality, but with an exquisite, aching tenderness, the firm, hard knowledge that she wants exactly what you want, though she might be too principled to admit it to herself.

To serve, without question, to obey: the grace that binds us and knows us.

"But what about Laura?" she'll say once she recovers herself. The tears filming her eyes will hurt and startle you, until you figure out that they're not for her, but for her sister. She wouldn't want to hurt Laura, particularly now, after all she's been given.

"I love her," you'll say. And you'll mean it of course. With all your heart and mind, the wholeness of your past and what's to come.

"But where? How?"

And you'll surprise her, because you'll be surprising yourself, no inkling of what you have in mind, because you haven't even dared to go there imaginatively, not really. For if you thought about it too clearly, the pain of it, the absence of Laura in your life, would break you in two.

And the absolute worst that could happen?

She'll look at you with pity, maybe the faintest trace of contempt behind her smile. She'll pat your arm the way she'd pat a harried, panting dog, who spends night after night hiding beneath a parked car. But even if that's the case, she'll respect you for having told her the truth. And who's to say that she won't toss and turn at night, and tell you something different the next time you're standing together in the kitchen, tearing spinach leaves apart?

Simple as that, my friend. Are you listening to me? And all will be well.

•

"I'll see you there tonight," Laura said. Her face looked partly hopeful, as if she were interested, for the first time in months, in heading off for the store. In the last few weekends, the sidewalks of Ocean Ridge had been busy—people threading in and out between newly installed lanterns. But Laura's hope felt larger than the three of us, than everything inside the room, or out the window.

"What's gotten into you?" I said, spreading blackberry jam on a piece of rye toast. As far as I could tell, I had a great big smile on my face.

"What?" Laura smiled too.

"Oh, I don't know. You. You're in this beautiful mood. You must be feeling good. Is that right?"

Laura shrugged herself into the arms of her yellow windbreaker. She looked off to the right, through the window, as if some meaning could be pulled in from the acidic spring green of the leaves. Then she pulled her attention back into the room. "You goof." She leaned down to kiss me. It wasn't the quick familial kiss we usually gave each other upon good-bye, but a kiss I'd almost forgotten. It wanted to make contact, lushly, with a little wet in it.

"Where will I meet you?" I rubbed her face with my napkin. The slightest hint of yolk smeared her eyetooth.

"I might be there after eight. I'll keep an eye out, but you should save a seat. Grab me a place on the far, far left." Laura looked at me a little funny, cloudy in her right eye. She held onto the back of my chair. "Bye, dear," she said thickly. She looked to Joan, who stood at the counter, whispering the evening's speech aloud to herself. "You're not nervous...."

"Me?" Joan said, glancing up, startled.

Laura shook her head, flipped her hand. "You're going to be a powerhouse. I can already feel you burning down that podium." And she blew comically at the tips of her fingers, then looked to me, so that I had no choice but to shake my head in agreement. "See you," I mouthed back.

I sat at the kitchen table while the car engine clicked and caught and murmured away, until the sounds of the house—cooling system, re-frigerator, dehumidifier, computer—lulled me with their snowy calm. Across from me, Joan brushed her hair with such force that I was fasci-nated that it didn't tear at the roots. *Easy, girl.*

"You know she's right," said Joan reproachfully.

I looked down at my emptied plate. The yellow from the busted yolks looked deadly, a little vicious, difficult to clean.

"I don't know why I feel this good. Ridiculously good. Do you think I should be worried about that?"

I tried my best to keep my face free. Truth be told, talk like this wor-ried me. Back when I went through my boxing phase I'd end up on my ass every time I walked into the ring with too much step, too much brio. I needed that doubt or I'd be done. But that didn't mean I thought that *she* should think such shit.

"I think you know you're going to win, and I think you know it deep down. It's not like you don't have all the facts on your side."

"You're telling me the truth?" she said, with a puzzled expression, edging on a smile.

"Why are you smiling?"

"I'm smiling?"

I craned back in my chair and burst out laughing, the tiniest shred of egg spraying from the space between my back teeth. *Great, chump.*

"Stop!" she said, and slapped me. The slap alarmed me, coming as it did, pulsing a little while, and hotly through my shoulder. "You know how I am. I'm convinced that I'm going to fall flat on my face if I'm not working twice as hard as everybody. But today it feels like I could just talk off the top of my head. And I'd be convincing and real because . . . Isidore, I'm not even going in there with any notes."

I felt trusted, enlivened to her. I loved this confiding in me, this call-ing me by my name. I didn't know I'd been asleep till this minute. Out the window, the yellow berries on the firethorn looked crisp and liquid, as if telling me: here I am.

"I have something to tell you."

"Oh, God," Joan said, and laughed, the skin at the base of her throat blushing upward to her face. Even the pinpoint moles beside her eye looked clever and new. "I do, too."

I stilled myself. No one in the world had kept himself so still, not someone in 1875, waiting to have his picture taken. Not someone standing in front of a firing squad, on the furthest side of the world.

To serve, without question, to obey: the grace that binds us and knows us.

Then Richard was in the kitchen, face bright with color. Dressed in an electric blue double-breasted suit with wide labels and pant legs— too loud, if you asked me, for anything as dour as a meeting. How long had he been standing there? He didn't so much as look us in the eye, but at the fact of us together at the table. I looked down at my white, V-neck T-shirt. It struck me as more gray than white now, having been washed with navies and blacks too many times.

"What's this, some freaking dancehall?"

"We're coming!" Joan said, leaping to her feet.

•

The planning board chairman banged the gavel two minutes ahead of schedule. She struck me as preoccupied, tetchy, everything about her hastily put together: the seams of her black blouse crooked, the middle button undone to reveal an oval of freckled white skin beneath her breasts. For some reason, Richard and Amy chose to sit two rows behind Joan and me. They flipped through pages of notes, and made a grand show of scribbling, of hushed exchange, sending out intimidation from their little pocket of the room.

The flagpole, the podium, the town seal, the state seal. The hard chairs, the soft chairs, the white walls, the baseboards. The carpet with its thick black gash repaired with duct tape. The glassed-in map of

Dunbarton Township with its many-colored pinheads. The framed portraits of former mayors along one wall, with all the sexual vividness of nineteenth-century spinsters looking back at us from the realm of the dead. A calming smell of peppermint wafted through the hall, as if someone, fearing riot, sprayed it ten minutes prior to the meeting.

Joan sat straight, impossibly straight, eyes keyed on everything ahead of her.

But things went well, exceedingly well. At least for us. A person got up, testified against the project, a person sat down. A person got up, testified against the project, a person sat down. There were props, reports, maps, handouts, exhibits, photos, diagrams printed in multiple colors, slicker and more appetizing than a plate of chicken parmagiana (not that I ever touched the stuff) on a supermarket circular. If only they weren't so well behaved about it. The defeat of the townhouses? Absolutely, yes; I could stand beside that, but the words, the empty, weary formulas of those words? No. I hated hearing all that belief processed and refined, beaten to something like Quaker Instant Oatmeal. Why couldn't someone simply jump to his feet, cry out, wave his arms above his head? I thought of doing it myself, for Christ's sake, if I didn't think it would rot our chances. Not to mention Joan pulling me down by the arm with a hiss.

I thought of the parking lot of a few minutes back. The party atmosphere of it: trading jokes and lighting one another's cigarettes. That kind of fakery I could deal with. Good manners were one thing. Fakery about the life-and-death sort of thing was another. And this was one life-and-death sort of thing, not fakey-fakey.

A sleepy, queasy feeling came over me. It was the kind of feeling I had when I slapped my back packet for my wallet, and finding it there, almost felt a twinge of disappointment, for the loss of it would have centered me, pumped up my heartbeat, given me a purpose.

Then that feeling was gone, as if I'd been caught inside a net, the net lifted to the surface—all muddy, clotted with barnacles and mussels and seaweed—but no me.

Joan sat on the edge of her seat, poised to stand. She glanced in my direction, wobbled her mouth a bit, lifted the left side of her face, then her right. She stood, clutching her folder to her chest, and walked briskly to the stage, her shoulders dropped, her butt tucked in, just the way I'd told her to walk.

She held onto the sides of the podium. She looked out at the crowd with—not authority. Not exactly that, but something infinitely more interesting: a genuine desire to help. She didn't speak for a moment, which only urged us toward her. Who couldn't have been proud of her? There wasn't a single person in that room who couldn't have been impressed because she had the look of someone who knew the repercussions of these proposals, at least for some. She wasn't another person who didn't want her view blocked, or hated change. She still knew the possibility of living in a motel down the street, or worse, in one of those peeling wooden arcs up on blocks, down by the marina, should something ever go wrong in our house.

Not that I intended to let that happen. Or Laura.

When did I sense it? I saw it rattle through her, flutter her eyelids. Was it when she started speeding up, attacking the beginning of her sentences with a false style that ran out on her before she needed another breath? Or was it her posture? She stood with all her weight on one foot, the other crossed behind her. Her shoulders rolled forward and down, as other pressures rose to the surface. I did my best to anchor myself in my seat, to look like she was saying the most critical things of the night. Which was true, no doubt in my mind, but I wanted the people seated behind me to see it. I wanted to do it in such a way that it didn't call attention to me or prompt them to think: *That torch he's holding is going to set the room afire; run for your little lives.*

She kept on going, painfully, deliberately, woodenly. She was standing outside of herself, watching herself the way we were watching her. She kept reaching for the right word (and I was reaching there along with her), but the harder she tried, the more elusive it was, so just as she almost touched it (beautiful, generous thing), it swam away: a sunfish she'd been trying to grip with her bare hands. Of all the pains in the world, the worst has got to be watching the humiliation of someone you care about. If there was something I could have done—God, my God: ten times over and more. I would have broken the glass of the fire alarm; I would have walked up to her with a Dixie cup and two Diazapam; I would have stood up there myself, in spite of my high school public speaking class, when I stood ten full minutes in front of the room, lockjawed, unable to talk.

Twenty years ago, on the same stage from which I heard my wife sing so flawlessly, so convincingly, a visiting poet stood before our school assembly. He still haunted me. His voice, so quickly exhausted, still woke me up some nights, though I can't even remember his name, or a single line of his work. Although he was known for bringing audiences of all stripes and sorts to their feet, he clearly hadn't realized that his better days were behind him. He started with a joke. Nobody laughed. It wasn't a bad joke. Only that he might have been speaking in a private language to us. Soon he was saying things like, "If you didn't like that, how about this one." But the more he begged for our attention, the more we refused to give it to him. The more he told us we didn't want him, the more we agreed to play that part, with panache and a little cruelty. By the time he'd announced the two-poem mark, people were routinely getting up to go to the bathroom, sandals spanking the floor. And wouldn't you know that once he finished, he walked across the stage, walked down the steps, and sat in the empty chair beside me. He put his hand on my leg, as if to say, at least I have you in the room.

And now Joan was doing that as well. She left the stage. She stood before me; she put her hand on my knee as she sat, claiming me.

"You were great," I whispered, leaning in toward her until our heads butted.

Joan shook her head, as if she were trying to shake herself out of the room.

"Really," I said.

"That was shit," she said plainly, loud enough to be heard by the first two front rows. A woman in a paisley cap and pale skin screwed up her face . . . in agreement or dismay? I couldn't tell.

I nodded, emphatically.

"I didn't get to say a third of what I wanted to say."

"What you did was fine. It was better than fine. What am I saying? You were fucking awesome." Awesome: a word I'd never used before in my life, baggy word, useless, a kid word I'd never believed in.

And the look on her face was a wince that wouldn't stop. She looked like an ice skater who had landed on her ankle in an awful way. She kept saying she was fine; yes, she could still walk on it. No, it wasn't sprained. She stared at the flagpole on the stage, an odd smile trying to break though that look, but I knew she was shaken deep inside.

I held Joan's hand for the next hour and a half. Moist and cold: it made me think of Laura's hand on the night she'd claimed to have fallen in the store. The truth is, I didn't hear any of it, and I didn't care to. You didn't have to be Bertrand Russell to figure out that the mathematics had shifted in the room. The developers' representatives stood before the crowd with tapered suits, scrubbed faces, and dazzling maps in every shade of the spectrum. But that wasn't what worked on us. They talked like they might be doing us a kindness. Of all the communities on the coast they had chosen us, not only for our sense of order and beauty, but because we were decent people. They didn't invoke anything about the American dream or patriotism; they were too smart for that. They simply anticipated everything that people wanted to hear and said it better. Now, for instance, they spoke of the supreme quality of wildlife in our lagoons. The swift and subtle least tern (slide, slide,

slide, slide). The dainty, inquisitive egret (slide, slide, slide, slide). The box turtle. You get the picture. I glanced over my shoulder, practically turning around in my seat, to see whether Laura had come in. Even the most cynical and hard-bitten in the group half-nodded in assent, their shoulders relaxing, in spite of themselves. I even found them working on me, as much as I hated every word of it. They praised Lumina for its singularity, its uniqueness. They ensured us that it was worthy of surgical preservation, and with their superior resources and skills (and capital!) they asked for our permission to participate in their love for the place.

To my right Joan sat looking straight ahead, a weary, dizzied smile, as if she were being wheeled into intensive care.

It was almost eleven o'clock when Richard and Amy went up separately before the group. They were in tremendous form, however; no small feat after what they'd followed. Somehow they'd managed to keep up their energy. There was even a basic radiance about them; their voices relaxed, tinged with optimism. But everyone beside me and around me looked tired. Their backs must have hurt. They kept shifting in their seats; they scratched; they coughed nervous coughs that triggered other nervous coughs. How could anybody entertain the consequences of a plan that was years in the future when their mouths were stale and they were worried about setting the alarm clock for work? People could only take in so much information before it turned to milk shake in their brains.

Finally, three minutes after midnight, the chairman made her announcement:

"We'll continue this discussion in two weeks." Bang of gavel.

Then I saw it: the chairman's barest glance toward the developers' representatives. Nothing obvious, mind you, but a look of concern. It didn't say: *detachment*.

Joan and I stayed put in our seats, not speaking, not moving, as the crowd filed past us toward the back. A tall black man with taut forearms and a confusingly slack stomach started folding up the extra chairs, talking to himself in a Caribbean lilt.

Outside, the night was warm, humid, spiky with current. Severe thunderstorms in the forecast? Unlikely groups paired off: Honey and Harry, Ferris and Bess Helen Graver. They all took note of us walking to the car, but I knew it well enough from the gym or from the playing field: no one wanted a loser.

An incredible gust blew off the bay, and a tired *ah* rose upward from the crowd. Hands pushed in pockets; coats pulled tighter around shoulders; hair blew out of buns and pigtails and weaves until everyone stood starched and a little dazed.

Halfway across the parking lot, footsteps hurried at our backs. I ushered Joan along, lest someone throw something at us. Not that I believed it would happen, but the skin felt strange on the back of my neck. Something was out there, alive.

"Thank you, Joan," Amy said.

"Terrific job," said Richard. He said it with such exceeding blandness that it was impossible not to hear his disappointment. He extended his hand to Joan, like a pastor on the steps of a church.

"You too," Joan said.

"We have our work cut out for us," said Richard, turning not to Joan or Amy but to me. He looked at me fully in the face for the very first time, as if it were less stressful to deal with an unknown quantity than with the person who had worked yet failed to win his approval. I zipped up my jacket while looking at him eye to eye. What did he want from me? I had nothing to give, and yet he seemed to know something beyond the limits of my grasp. *Go ahead*, I thought. *Try me.* Which must have hardened my face. He looked back to Joan.

"We presented a very strong case," Richard added.

Joan nodded. She offered a little smile, making sure not to look directly at anyone.

I said, "In two weeks, they're all going to be disgusted with themselves for even giving this stupid project the time of day."

"That's what we want to hear," said Joan.

"Hear, hear," Richard said.

"Get some sleep, all," I said, raising an imaginary toast.

"He's right," Richard said, looking around at the two women, who, remembering they were in competition, seemed to try to outdo each other, through the shine of their attention to him. "Let's get some sleep."

"Good night." And the chorus of good nights traded back and forth as the car doors slammed shut, and the engines coughed and clicked and went running.

Inside the truck, Joan pressed her forehead against the passenger window. She put such pressure on the glass that I imagined it falling out, splintering onto the pavement. Her breath fogged the window till it made rainbows of the streetlights, blurring out the branches and the leaves. I thought of us suspended underwater: fish looking upward through red tide.

She said, "Did you see the look on his face?"

"He's tired," I said, "Sit tight. You'll see it differently tomorrow."

"I'm never going to forget that expression." She started picking at the hole in the black vinyl seat. I would have told anyone else to lay off, but I let her pick away. She might have been mauling a pissed-on mattress dropped off along a curb, not the truck that I'd known and loved.

On the other side of the trees, a tall bearded man stole across the town park as if he held something expensive that wasn't his.

"How could that have happened?"

"Have a mint." I picked up a tired half roll of Life Savers from the coin tray. She waved it off.

"Why can I sound like I know what I'm talking about one minute and be so clueless the next?" Then she reached for the mints herself, coiled down the foil wrap. She passed not one, but two across her bottom lip. "I just want to do some good while I'm still around."

"You are doing good. You're doing great."

She clicked the Life Savers against her front teeth. "I'm doing shit."

"This isn't your last night on Earth. Give yourself a rest, you're stressed out. You're talking like you're going to die first thing tomorrow morning."

"How do *you* know that? How do I?"

"You can't live that way. You can't put that kind of weight on things. We'd never get out of bed. I mean, roads wouldn't get built, poems wouldn't get written. Prayers. Abstract paintings—Jesus."

It seemed amazing that we were able to talk like this. I expected us to be shouting, slamming down our hands until we broke bones against the dashboard. But we were hushed, reasonable.

"It's just like—" Joan breathed here, and held it, as if that breath were something endangered, cherished. "You go through this small rushed life trying to do your best for something. You try and you try, and of course it breaks you."

I felt my brows lift, in spite of me.

"What?"

"Obviously," I muttered, "there's nothing I can say."

She looked down at the dashboard lights with a relaxed mouth. She chewed up the last of her mints and swallowed. "How much gas does this thing use?"

"What are you saying?"

She shook her head back and forth, pain screwed into her smile. The slightest sag beneath her chin made me think of her at sixty, still beautiful but with her hair dyed. I tried not to think of it, that brassy, unflattering color against her skin.

I gunned the ignition. What could I have said to her? What more could I have done without indicating the dank, sorry truth: that I wanted her to stop it this instant because she was making me feel helpless. She had a right to feel like shit. She had a right to think her worries were real. And I had a right to tell her to keep her goddamn hands off my truck. It wasn't her problem that I came up short when it came to trying to help. But none of that would change if we stayed put. We needed to shake us loose from this parking lot, this location. I thought of Sandy Hook, all those hot city lights rosing the sky across New York Harbor. I thought of Point Pleasant Beach, Seaside Heights, Wildwood. Or Coney Island: that would take care of it. Although the streets could be dangerous, we'd park beside the boardwalk. We'd get out, step over bottles and weeds, and we'd be entirely there, away from the wants that were harming us. We'd walk right by the gangs, knowing we were their wards now: blessed and protected. Later, after a few rounds at Faber's Fascination, we'd go to Joey's Clams and order two hot dogs each. We'd eat standing, elbow to elbow with all sorts of people we'd never come across anywhere else: a man in a sailor's cap made with newspaper, a boy whose neck was so loaded with chains that they'd left dark green stains on his skin.

Just as I shifted into reverse, a man stood at the window, so close that the skin on my neck grabbed. The smell of animal fear came off my shirt. Though his eyes were open and young, gray glistened in his beard.

Where did I know him from?

Of course, then: The man running across the park!

Joan closed her eyes, face toward the windshield. She moistened her lips. "I'll talk to you tomorrow," she said, wrenching upward on the door handle.

"What are you talking about?"

"This was what I was going to tell you."

"You've lost me."

"This is Saskia," she said. "I told you about Saskia, didn't I? Richard's sister's son?"

"Yes?" I said, asking for more. I looked at his curiously open face, grinning and a little mad. But wasn't it him? That's right, wasn't he the boy she led from house to house, where I sat from my little perch, in somebody else's window?

So on and on they went, right in front of my face, and my refusal to see.

"Thank you," she said, patting me on my knee, looking at me directly now. She kissed the tips of two fingers then pressed them briefly, against my throat, before taking them away.

"You're getting out," I said plainly.

She shook her head. I looked down to see that I was holding her hand too hard. If I held it any harder she wouldn't be able to use it for days. I let go.

"Would you like me to wait?"

I expected disgust in her face, but no. "I know what I'm doing."

She opened the door. I knew that face, that walk too well. It knew that everything was wrong with what it was about to do. It didn't respond to reason. It knew it was shameful; it knew it was indifferent; it didn't care about the people upon whom it befell. It wanted to be thrown up against a wall. It wanted its face rammed down into a pillow. It didn't want to breathe. No, it wanted to choke. That urge to shake off the container of your skin, your life. It made absolute sense to me. I saw it, I yearned for it, I wanted some of it for myself.

She sat beside him in the front seat of his car. They sat there, no exchange of touches or words. Then they drove off, turning onto the northbound lanes of Route Nine with surprising caution and respect.

I sat behind the steering wheel of the pickup until mine was the only car left in the parking lot.

I touched the spot on my throat where she touched me, as I once felt for mumps, years back, in grade school.

The headlights lit up the tree ahead, its limbs so wide and profound it seemed to spite and defy me. I placed my finger inside the hole on her seat. Instantly, I tore it through and stopped only when my finger burned. I brought it to my lips, tasting. It hurt like hell, now that I'd twisted my knuckle.

I pulled out onto the highway. I thought about how hard we work for what we think we want. We do everything we need to do: we work ourselves silly; we stay up half the night, toiling because it's what we think we want. But things have already been set up for us. Joan, of all people, should have known that by now. Not that I thought that she wanted to cede Lumina to the developers, but whatever she wanted, it didn't involve standing in front of a crowd. I'm not even sure she wanted to save her mother. Those choices were already made for you, were always larger than your ability to control. They weren't something that you decided upon, as much as you needed to trick yourself into thinking otherwise. Ask her mother.

•

I walked through the cemetery, in and out between the monuments. Some were higher than my head, others barely touching my knee, all in a row, all impossibly orderly. Darker than I'd expected. No streetlights at this distance, and the flashlight beam so weak I could barely see my shoes. I kicked a rock—or was it a skull? A planter on its side. I squatted, then, replanted the geraniums inside it, the petals so browned now and creamy, I imagined them melting on my tongue.

Up a little knoll, then down into a dell, grassy and thick. I couldn't tell it was this row or the next, though none of the names looked familiar: CHIANESE, CORTESE, CHIUSANO, CANUSO. Beautiful Italian names, musical, their letters likely stippled orange-gold and green if only I could see. I turned right, left, right again. Night smells filled the air: wet earth and plants dripping with sprinkler water, a faint smell of marsh-bed in the distance, fecal. The texture of the ground beneath my feet changed minute to minute: newly planted grass, soil just raked, none of it as flat and tended as I'd expected. A little loamy. It occurred to me that I was turning this part of the cemetery into a ruin, and some poor gus would be out here, if not tomorrow, then the next day, shaking his head, trying to fix up my damage before his supervisor came by in his truck.

And then my flashlight went dead. I shook it. The batteries rattled as if I were shaking a can of spray paint.

I walked and walked, cursing my personal idiocy. A tree dropped something on my head: a spider, a seed pod? My shoes so wet from the dew that they squeaked. They weren't so far from falling apart, really, sole separating from the rubber. Suddenly, more than anything, I wanted to be anywhere else. It didn't matter if I came out at the west gate. It didn't matter if I came out at the north, where I'd have to walk a full half-mile, down the slope to the street, around the fence posts to the car. It didn't even matter if I had to take the bus or hitchhike. Anything to get away from the dead. I looked up at the sky for guidance, but there was no guidance for me. No planets or moon, just a wisp of high clouds, lit sodium-gold by the lights of town. A crow flew from tree to tree to browning bush. Then, just as the sweat started beading my neck, I lay belly-down on the ground, pressed my ear against the soil, so chilly and moist and unyielding. My jacket would be stained when I stood up, but I didn't need this jacket anyway. I'd leave it for somebody to take. And all the things I could have been asking, "Where did you go, Mama? Why did you do what you did to Joan?"—none of it mattered beyond the moment. "Help us," I said, mouth pressed to the ground.

•

Fifteen miles away, at the same moment, in a one-story motel off the highway, Saskia was driving into Joan with such force, that she felt the headboard being driven into the wall. And she couldn't help but push back. No tenderness between them, no heads tossed back in laughter, but that wasn't what they wanted. They were there to work.

Suddenly I am the person . . . I am the person who is fucking and being fucked, and all the lights go out, and it's just me, freed from time and space, remembering the man I'd been.

CHAPTER 9

I didn't bother to park around the corner or down the street. I pulled up into the driveway, stopped at the garage door, as if I'd always belonged here. I slammed shut the door. My boots shocked the pavement, echoing against the neighbors' house. There was no question of my being seen. The time was three in the morning.

I rapped on the storm door, waiting. The water in the lagoon plopped and slapped. Pulleys squeaked. Ropes rubbed against eyelets. I knocked again and again. Was she really asleep? Come on now. And what about the baby—why hadn't she started to cry? At my feet, a load of *Shopper's Guides* in their blue plastic protection. Weeds leached over the edges of the sidewalk, and only then did I realize that the lawn service hadn't come by in weeks. I'd cut it myself, in the morning, just as the kids were walking to school, my ski mask pulled down over my face.

I walked around to the side. My sneakers so wet now that I took them off, dropped them by the hose bib. Better the cold wet grass on my feet than that spongy crumble. I tapped lightly on her bedroom window, then harder. The light went on next door. In the time it took me to sing *Happy Birthday* twice to myself, I crouched there. Then the window went dark again.

I reached for the storm window frame. It slipped out easily, as easily as a skin. I pushed up on the regular window, no lock—what was she thinking? And then I lifted myself up by my arms. I held myself in place, straining my triceps until the burn felt good.

Even in the dark, I knew the furniture was gone. Nothing left behind, no castoff rags, no leftover boxes or window sprays or coat hangers. No books, no medicine bottles with safety caps, no gluey coins, crusted soap dishes, or tear outs from magazines. Stripped clean and final. As stainless as a death. I almost blessed it. And who would ever guess what had happened in this room? The adventures.

•

"Man!" the homeless fellow cried. "Man!"

I waited at the stoplight, no other cars behind me, and here's this guy coming up to my closed window, a face so lined with suffering and a wrecked kind of joy that he looks like some honored guest from the next world. How could a face come to look like that in a place where most of us didn't have to worry about paying the dental bill? His pants are laundered, as far as I can tell, though they're several sizes too large, hems shredding as they drag on the pavement. And here I am pushing down the clutch with my bare left foot, because I was too fucked up to pick up my shoes from Janet's yard.

A light breeze off the bay, from the south-southwest. It's three thirty-three in the morning, according to the man on the radio, who's solemn tonight, with a raspy drone like Leonard Cohen's. I tell the guy that. "It's three thirty in the morning."

"It's the best time," he says. "People are coming home from parties. People are drunk. People are generous, man. Saintly and generous."

I pull out my wallet. Inside are two twenties, and the coin tray is loaded with pennies, too many to give him; they'd only weigh down his pockets, and for what? The guy's face, though, is urgent, asking. Blood brushes his upper gum when he smiles.

"You're giving me twenty dollars?"

I say, "That's not enough?"

His mouth opens, and there it is: gum disease—the bare, bald fact of it—wafting in my truck like a bacterial curse. I try not to swallow, try not to turn my head from him.

"Here's another," I say, and give him everything I have as if it's a hold up.

The light turns green. I pull forward and catch him in my rearview. He walks to the sandy side of the road, shaking his head like I'm the asshole of the night.

•

She said, "I don't feel so good."

Laura was lying on her back on the living room sofa when I walked in the door, the afghan pulled up to her chin. The look of her skin was pale. "Oh, *babe*," I said, and put my palm to her forehead. This was no act: her back teeth clattered. She shook. She had a fever.

"I didn't make it to the meeting," she said, dried out, chapped.

"Don't worry about that," I said, rubbing and tugging on the fingers. "What can I do for you?"

"I tried to go, I tried, I'm not kidding you, but I felt so sick driving home." She closed her eyes, looked at the living room window, puzzled, as if the tide in the lagoon could rise up and leak in the house. "I even stopped for ten minutes at the rest stop. I took a nap. And when I woke up I thought I was back at the store."

The thought of her outside the squat brick building where the casino buses ran their engines at all hours, browning the leaves with pollution, broke my surface like a shoe through a lake. I envisioned my hands on Joan's face—then *Saskia's* hands—sweat soaking my shirt beneath the armpits. But we were talking about my wife here.

"Do you think Joan will hate me?"

"Joan will be fine. Do you want something to drink?" And I planted her forehead with a kiss.

It couldn't be back: *no.*

"I suppose," she said, mouth turning down. "But I wanted her to know I'm on her side." She pulled from my hand, looked away. She fingered the large tan button on the back of the sofa, like an ornery child, not the woman who spent weeks making sure it was the right sofa for the room.

The light outside the window went through stages: first the yellow of sugarless lemonade, then a pale, in-between color. Putty? Oyster?

Her skin smelled hot and unfamiliar, like a barnyard or dirtied feet. I thought of a single finger wiping out the inside of my stomach.

"Don't you think we should take you to the doctor?" I said after a pause.

"It's just the flu. I'm sure of it. I've had the flu before. Nothing new about the flu."

"But I'm just worried about . . . Why couldn't he put a name to it? Stupid doctor."

"This has nothing to do with any of it," she said, frowning, forcing her eyes shut. I must have gotten it from Madison, okay?"

"Laura—"

"Let it alone!" she cried, and it came out with such force that it clanked like a lid on a spaghetti pot. I pumped back, startled. This wasn't the way we'd talked to one another. This was my friend.

"How did it go?" she said after a long pause. Her voice was so quiet now I had to lean down over her face, turn my ear above her mouth.

"What?"

"The meeting."

"Not good. Well, at least that's what Joan thought." I shrugged, pushed the sweat off my temple with my open hand. It seemed pointless at this moment to say I saw it differently. Why say *spring* when the world is going up in flames in front of you?

Within seconds, she was completely out of it, her body giving in. I watched for a good while (her lank hair, her dried out lips) until the room went dark, and I couldn't watch anymore. What did God want from us? The question was ridiculous, but it wouldn't stop coming, relentless as a car alarm. What did God want from us? Not that I thought God was anywhere behind us or nearby, if there even was a God. But the absence of any answer was so keen and discernable that I might have run out the door, howling like a dog abandoned, head lifted in protest. Instead, I walked down the hall to the powder room. I shut the door behind me. The face that met me in the mirror wasn't my face. It was the face of an older man, my Uncle Moishe, or my father two weeks before he died. It was a helpless face; it had had enough, a rugged red, the pores so large you could slide needles through them. Where was my Laura now? I reached for a towel and stopped up my mouth—anything so she couldn't be bothered by my sounds: she had too much to think about now. I watched myself in the mirror, conscious of my tears, and hating my tears all at the same time. They ran into the corners of my mouth, tasting like rain. But still I kept choking, despite my intention to walk back to that room and be the kindness for her that I'd hoped to be.

Mystery disease. It did not belong in our house.

Then I replaced the towel on the rack. I wiped down the evidence of rinsed out mouths from the basin, shined up the faucet with a torn piece of Kleenex. I took in a breath, held it, and let it go. The inside of my chest felt gratified and sore as if I'd run six times to the bay and back again. Then I walked to the living room.

"What's wrong?" Laura said.

I shook my head, sniffed. She was sitting now, palms pressed down on the sofa, on either side of her, as if she needed to do that.

I handed the cup to her. "I love you, babe."

"Where's your shoes?" And she smiled as through she could see the map of my night—whole and entire—glowing bright green on the map of her imagination. She put her hand on my hand. The tops of my feet were nicked and split. They bled, as if I'd cut them on purpose.

•

I'd expected Joan to spring back up. I thought she'd be literally up and running the next morning, making phone calls. But it didn't work out like that. Instead Joan helped me help Laura get better. She made soup; she went to the health food store to pick up the powders and potions. It was a very healthy time in the house, each of us back in our pockets, our gorgeous, rightful places.

But soon the tasks ran out. When Joan wasn't at the caterer or helping me, she sat on the deck, hours at a time, and watched the lagoon. I'd have felt no concern if there was a look of belief on that face. Or flat-out sadness. But there was nothing on the inside of that face, and though that might have struck some as peaceful, I knew it wasn't peaceful. Could I have called it suspension? An endless Verrazano of the imagination, no way left and no way right, no dunes or marshlands in view, and even the planes overhead and the squid and the crabs were exactly what they were, nothing to *know*. Water shown upward like a mirror, flashing, where all she could see was her pitiable self.

Joan needed to do something again. To *attend*.

And how long would it be before she packed up her room?

One day, I stood in the bedroom, looking for a pair of black socks without holes. (They all had holes these days; they all gave out at the same time.) Laura and Joan were alone in the living room. I sensed that they'd thought I'd gone for a ride, as I'd walked out the back door, not five minutes before, to take out the garbage, the recyclables. A current might have ticked through the wall. If I could have, I would have made myself smaller, a sand burr, a puff of lint in a dish. I listened, as I might have listened twenty years back, when I crouched in my room as my father told Lily Gamble, the lady from Chilton Lane, that there would only ever be one woman in his life, and she was my mother, who was dead. He hadn't acknowledged that moment that my mother was really dead. And it had taken all of five years.

I readied myself for something I'd hate to hear. Something I'd hear ten years in the future, lying in bed in a stuffy room, my sinuses closing up.

Joan said, "Do you think it's time we took you to the doctor?"

The fourth day of Laura's illness. Her eyes had a little more life in them, but twice a day she went through a new change of clothes, having sweated through the previous, before her body went cold, shaking again. I imagined the hamper spilling over with T-shirts, tracksuits: all still damp, fecund, the troubling, rich scent of broth.

"You're not answering me," Joan said. "A doctor might help to get you through this."

If I weren't in such a bland mood myself, I would have kissed the back of my hand. Thank God that Joan was taking it on. I'd had enough of playing the policeman, the enforcer, and who's to say that that kind of thing doesn't set one against the other? Didn't I once say that my skin had started to taste like Laura's? And all Laura had done was love me, as God was said to do.

"You need to look out for yourself," Laura said, with perfect charity, as if she hadn't been sick since childhood.

"You're the one who's sick," Joan said.

"You're running yourself down," Laura said. "See that soup?"

Here I imagined Joan nodding, or simply staring blankly, a little rigid in her chin.

"I want you to go into the kitchen," Laura said, "find your favorite bowl, fill it up with soup."

"Can't I just reheat this one?"

"It's for you, silly, you," Laura said. "All I want's a hamburger, some fries. If only I felt well enough to drive."

There she was to me, the woman I saw on the stage, singing from her body, and somewhere not her. The curtains in the bedroom made a shifting motion, as if a child were wrapped inside them, playing I-see-you.

"Who's the one who's sick here?" Joan said.

"Don't look at me," Laura said. I heard a thrusting sound, as if a pillow were being punched to make a shape for the head.

"Why are you talking like this?" Joan said.

"Why are you asking questions you know the answers to?" Laura said.

"Thick!" Joan cried. "Thick! Thick! Thick! Thick!" And then I pictured a magazine flung, falling, its sheaves opening up to a face in a perfume ad, wafting a little scent into the room.

I walked back through the kitchen with an even heavier step, as if I'd just come back in from an errand. Joan sat at the table before an empty red bowl, pushing her dark hair back off her face. I pretended to rifle through the stack of mail, but it was a joke of mail: supermarket fliers and Mileage Plus and credit card offers. Outside, a blue jay cried in celebration.

"Everything okay?" I said to her.

"She hates me," Joan said, half serious, half joking.

"Loathes you," I said dully. I opened the refrigerator and hunted for a piece of cheese. I cut off a slice of cheddar and put it on a plate before her. Then I reached for an apple, Golden Delicious. The truth was, Joan seemed to have lost weight since the meeting: I could see it now, the stronger features, angular, almost manly. A certain sheen lost in the skin. I thought of a piece of fabric, a thin black cotton shirt, washed one time too many.

"Er," Joan said finally, with a rheumy smile.

"Er?" I said back. "Eat."

Joan crossed one eye, let the corner of her mouth squint. Still, she did as instructed. I perched on the edge of the chair, leaning forward, my fingers latched, thumb pressing against thumb until I pushed blood into the bottom halves.

"What about the townhouses?" I said.

"What about them?"

"Have you spoken to Richard?"

Joan chewed slowly, a little deliberately now, as if to show me how much effort she was expending on my behalf. A part of me wanted to pull her into the next room. Another part would have been happy never to see her face again.

"Don't you think you should call?" I said.

"He doesn't quite need me right now," Joan said.

"Where's your excitement?"

"I'm not sure I'm of very much use to him right now."

I coughed, out of disgust, which rolled into a real cough, rough and sanding, an abrasion in the throat. Warming tears sprang to my eyes.

Joan held up both hands. "Let me finish, okay? That's not defeat. That's not self-absorption."

"Self-absorption? *Joan*. I said nothing of the sort."

"I don't need your pity," she said, almost tender now, not unkind.

The sheer directness of her carved into my skin; I knew she saw the anger crackling through my face. I was a phone pole struck by lightning, a pot of water heated to boiling. I should have thrown her out the door, on her ass, on her heels. Instead, I walked out of the house, still blameless, offering no reply. I stood inside the garage and began to make an order of it: the hammers next to the pincers, the wire cutters next to the screwdrivers. The smells of grass seed, herbicide, rusty shovels wiped down with motor oil. Electrical cords wrapped and hanging on the hooks, as tidy as a display.

When she didn't come out to place a calming hand upon my back, I started all over again.

And where was Saskia? What was he doing this night of nights? Joan couldn't say a thing, for if she started, then what would come next?

I knew how to smell trouble when it came to lust. For example, our friend Carla, who after convincing us that the man she'd been dating for years was capable of cruelty, ended up walking down the aisle with him. Married, that's right. All the attempts at meals, kayak rentals, crabbing, picnics to the beach: we were never the same after that. There was her fear that we were thinking that she'd settled for something small and mean, and *our* sense that she resented us for suspecting that we thought such things. How could it be that the rope of us wouldn't fray?

Five days later Laura walked into the living room.

"All better!" she said.

Her face went flat, as if she were expecting me to walk up and hug her.

"All good," she said, more softly now.

I should have felt happy, but my stomach felt cramped, full, as if I'd eaten a loaf of wet, white bread. A life we'd put on hold was back again. Laura walked with a trepidation that belied the fact that health was a gift, something tentative and precious, a cough away from serious trouble. It was the way I'd felt after I'd had a terrific workout, and I'd met my body again. Vulnerable body, something I was only a guest in.

Two hours later, I felt a rough patch around the uvula, though I knew for sure I wasn't sick: I took my vitamins and supplements. I swallowed and talked myself out of swallowing again. But I didn't have it within me to stop. Mold, dehydration, pollen blown in from the roses: which of the three?

She'd been right all along. The flu.

•

I refused to lie in bed. I refused it just the way I refused to nap: it was never in my nature. Too much life to be missed by closing one's eyes and giving into nothing. But how belittling it was: the glands in the neck as hard as walnuts, the parched throat! And the smell. How could a human being, relatively clean and acquainted with soap, give off such a wretched, yellowy scent? If this was what Laura had endured, I would have picked up that hamburger myself. I would have bought her fresh popsicles, frigid and sweet, soothing those scraped membranes. And even if she'd eaten none of it upon my return, even if she didn't have the appetite she'd thought she did, I would have been perfectly fine with it. Anything to see her sitting up, waiting for me to come through the door with the bags of provisions under my arm.

I needed to get up to pee. The strength to muster such an undertaking seemed enormous, beyond my capacity. Hard to imagine I'd only been in the gym not two days before. I'd never get my body back again, but who the fuck cared?

The walls of the hall turned a grisly blue-black, the floor tipping like the floor of an amusement park ride.

"Easy," Laura said. She suddenly seemed to know more about good health than anyone.

"I'm okay."

She tried to guide me by the elbow. "Honey, you're a mess."

"I have to pee."

"Do you want me to help you?"

"What are you going to do, hold it for me?"

Her face emptied, blanched. Actually, I hadn't meant to bark it out.

"You could do that yourself," she said kindly. She opened the bathroom door and closed it, harder than she needed to.

In truth I could have used the help. I sprayed the rim, the floor, the walls, anywhere but where it was supposed to go. But I needed to rid myself of the useless poisons inside me, and when I could produce no more, I was surprised my feet didn't literally lift off the tile on account of my lightness.

Laura stood in the hallway, arms crossed, one shoulder higher than the other.

"Get to bed!" she said, pointing.

"Who are you?" I rasped.

"Laura Pompoleo-Mirsky, thank you very much."

She looked past me at the dribbling I'd made on the toilet seat.

"You didn't put the seat up? Jesus."

Now I couldn't keep my eyes open. I weaved a little and slumped against the wall. I wondered whether I was going to throw up.

"Marriage," she said cryptically, though not without sweetness.

I did as I was told, but I couldn't stay put. The room went hotter, as if a small hearth were burning inside the chest of drawers. I tossed and turned; I tore off my jockey shorts. Not five minutes later a sly band of canaries started fluttering in the room, wings flapping the ceiling, as if they were trying to flap through it. They were in my hair. They were slapping my groin. One even perched beside my lips, where it lay an impeccably neat turd, fragrant as an almond. Hard as I tried, I couldn't flick it away. The flapping went louder, the noise of their wings sweeping like brooms.

When I blinked, the room was only a room again.

"Laura," I called. "LAURA!"

So loud I'm sure I could have been heard down the street, the lagoon, the wooded side of Route Nine, and the industrial park. I looked at the window. The pane was dark, though I could have sworn the day had only begun. How had it gotten dark when I thought I was here, trying to pay attention?

She didn't appear. Of course she didn't appear just when I needed her most. But was it ridiculous to ask to hear her sing? Not that she'd done such a thing in years. But if there was ever time for it, the time was now, and I didn't even care if she had to turn her face to the wall, out of shyness of me, or dread. I didn't care if her voice was nasal and out of shape. Just as long as she lifted that wave: old, old soul, not her and not me, but somewhere behind us and beyond.

I called out her name again, this time quieter, as if I'd already sensed the futility of it. I did it to hear myself speak. Then, attached to the lampshade on the end table, a Post-it note.

Went out to the store for a few items. Call me if you need anything. Will be back in half hour. ♫

I closed my eyes, opened them, and closed them again. I sat up. I walked to the kitchen, steady now, solid on my two feet, and reached for the keys on the coat rack. I was tired of being locked up for the day, a boy home from school, no clue as to how his life would turn out.

CHAPTER 10

The truck felt like a new truck, the stick shift sliding from second gear to third, effortless and sexy. It didn't so much matter that my head wanted to be on another body: so hot and stark and cracked open at the temple. The world looked stranger, more vivid than I'd remembered: sprinklers chinked, twisting long, clear ropes of water on the yards. A boy on a skateboard—arms outstretched, eyes glazed—weaving in and out before my lights. I was definitely on my way to health again, when I failed to turn the wheel, and then it went down: an ugly rumbling and a scrape.

I was up on someone's yard. The pitch pine glowered before my truck: brooding, monstrous, beastly. I backed up onto the street and walked out. I'd knocked over a segment of the fence, the front tires bumping up and over a railroad tie. I crouched over, wretched, but nothing came up on my tongue. No acid or bile. No surprise: I couldn't even touch those sausage links at breakfast.

I looked around: no dog walkers, no strollers, no souls in sight. It wasn't a trash night. Still, I heard those skateboard wheels, distant now, banging the pavement where the streetlights couldn't reach.

Not two seconds after I was back on the road, the phone rang—that grating, twinkly jingle! Should I bother to answer? I wanted to throw it out the window and watch its batteries bouncing out its back.

"You're up." Laura's voice was barely there, as if a rag had been stuffed down her throat.

"I can hardly hear you."

"You didn't answer the other phone. I just assumed you were asleep."

It almost came out of my mouth: *Then why call? Has it come to spying on me?* Instead, I focused on the road ahead, the double yellow line. I said, "I didn't have enough energy to make it to the kitchen."

A tapping, as if she were standing right inside that kitchen, breaking eggs on the rim of her mother's glass bowl. Could she be? *Nada.* Wrong.

"You don't sound like yourself."

"Explain."

"You sound funny. Is something the matter with you?"

Well, you sound funny too. So formal and thick, as if you've just met me for the first time. As if you're afraid you're going to hear something so killing that you'll lose me for good. Always afraid of disruption, disturbance. Just like your husband. Risk it, darling. I'm here for you.

"I'm sick, Laura."

I felt her thoughts burrowing, deep inside my knowing. *Are you home, Isidore? Are you with some woman, passing on your sickness? Tell me now, let's be real: are you screwing the living daylights out of her?*

"What would you like me to get you?" she said, softly now. "Anything?"

The distance in her voice: I wanted to reach across for it until it loved me back. *What's wrong?* she'd say to my arms around her waist, my kisses to the back of her head and her neck.

Off the top of my head, I gave her a list, so effortless and genuinely like me, that I felt like I'd rehearsed it years ago for just this moment.

How much time did I have, five minutes? Ten? The time it took the cashier to scan the barcode on every item at checkout. The time it took to drive from the store down Route Nine to home: add that. Give or take five minutes to stop for gas, a newspaper, a bottle of mineral water. I turned left onto Panorama Way, right on Luxor, another right on Thunderbolt. The Blatherwick house soared, all floodlights and grand peaks, soffits glistening and recently stained. I reached for my keys and stepped outside. I breathed in the smells of the night: new mulch and salt hay. I walked up the stone walk, threading in and out through glossy, expensive plants. Ridiculous walk, built with cut stone trucked in from some cash-strapped place: Appalachia, Western Maryland, Western Pennsylvania, God help us all.

There she was: Joan with her brain in me!

Someone cried nearby. At first I was sure it was in reaction to a slap, so sad and profound in its woundedness. I flinched, locked my knees, as if fighting off the impulse to run. Then a moan, so gorgeous, low-down, and familiar that I almost missed it: two people having sex, in the second floor bedroom of the house next door. Voices stopped cold. An anxious laugh, with a giggle, stopped up with a sheet. *Keep on, keep on,* I wanted to say. What would I have told them if they'd happened to see me standing here: that some man, a little sick in both body and brain, needed them to remind him why he was still alive?

I slugged the key into the lock. I wiggled it, but the dead bolt didn't let go. I stopped and tried it again. Strange: never once a problem in the dozen times I'd inspected this house. Then the dawning of a clear, sad fact: Jack Blatherwick had had the locks changed without handing over the new key.

I unhooked the hanging basket of impatiens and smashed it against the sidelight. No questions, no qualms. I stuck my arm through the open hole—*yee ha!*—then reached around for the knob and twisted left. I pulled out, held my wrist up close to my face. As far as I could tell, I hadn't cut myself: My skin all in one piece. Think of it, having to drive to the hospital with blood sliming my hands, my pants, my shirt, my truck!

I flipped on the foyer light, ran up the steps, two at a time. So swift I'd almost forgotten my fever. Another switch flipped, and I was inside the study, the same study I'd walked through, tentative and wary, with Joan not two weeks before. I pulled at the drawer of the file cabinet. The folders were thick, loaded. Papers, memos, maps, phone bills, construction codes: no time for particulars. But I took one and then another, and still another, certain for sure she'd find exactly the needed thing.

I was out of there before the dread came. But even before that, I cleaned up the broken pot, the spilled soil with its foamy white crumbs. I put what was left of the impatiens in my coat pocket, now heavy with dirt. I'd replant the flower much later in our own garden, beneath the mimosas.

•

And there I was, not in the middle of my life, but somewhere else, so frightening, that I can't even tell how fast it happened:

I'm eight. I'm in the Strathmore Acme, my father and Uncle Moishe in the next aisle—their loud, dry voices carrying over the shelves.

"Matzoh ball or minestrone?"

"Who wants soup?" Moishe says. "I hate soup!"

In that caustic, familial way that isn't even fighting at all. A box of nosedrops sits to my left. I hate nose drops, everything about them: that high stinging behind the uvula, the burning flood inside your sinuses. And they cheat you, they do! One second you're breathing, the next it's worse than before, your head so achy, your mucous membranes so impervious that you have all the breathing power of an English bulldog.

Still, I need them. I need that little blue box more than I need anything in the world. More than my mother back, more than my dog, Ashes, who ran away for good after I'd forgotten to shut the gate. My need is so great that I'm practically sick with it: already an adult smell is coming off my shirt, like milk gone bad. I hate it, because I'm not ready to lose who I am, which already feels like something earned, something I paid for.

I look to my left; I look to my right. The father and the uncle talking louder, and it's all I can do not to cry, I want it! I want it! Instead, I slip the nose drops in my coat, as if I'd been doing it all along, then walk to the front, past the checkers and the clerks, whom I eye on the way out. I stand outside by the front door, with my shoulders rolled forward, and my hands in my pockets, turning that little box over and over like a charm. Just long enough not to miss parting with it, at least somewhat. I put the nose drops in the first shopping cart in the locked train. I look at the little box while I wait for Uncle Moishe and my father. I feel bad for it and I want to crush it all at the same time. I want to flatten it with my shoe. Then the school librarian walks by, chin a little raised, eyes turned away from me, as if she's never seen me in my whole life, nor helped me with a question. She pulls the cart from the train. And in she goes with the box, which she'll no doubt buy, when she checks out, and she'll wonder what it's doing there when she gets home and unpacks the bags on her kitchen counter.

Within the next month, from various stores, I'll have stolen the following things: a camel-colored pencil case, a bag of multicolored eraser tips, some QT self-tanning cream, a foldout map of Middlesex County. Sometimes they end up in a shopping cart, sometimes they end up in the culvert behind Cambridge Park School, but never at home, and never anywhere where I could use them, need them, see them.

And then I stop. One day I tell myself it's time to stop. And I'm faithful to that promise to myself. I'm good. I never do it again. Till now.

Imagine it, a man like me, still thinking about his grade school years.

•

Keep me in you, I said, as I pulled up in front of the house. Keep me in you, I said, promise of a better ending. Keep me in you, I said, Laura, Joan. Even Mama, ashes in a jar. Keep me in you. Keep me in you.

●

I was under the comforter when Laura came in the house. The change was immediate in her face: the color deepening, the corners of her mouth relaxing. I was where I'd said I was. She passed me some grape-fruit segments, some rhubarb yogurt, a walnut muffin. (Where was the protein?) I knew I couldn't finish it, but I was actually starving after my little outing. I hadn't eaten all day, and the fact that she'd anticipated everything I wanted filled me with—what? Can I say it? Cracked ela-tion? My lips hummed in gratitude as she sat beside me on the bed, her arms halfway in her jacket sleeves.

We stilled ourselves for a good, long while, listening to the sounds of the clear, cool night outside the window.

Early the next morning I placed the folders on Joan's table, beside her computer beneath a paperweight. She was already out at her cater-ing job, probably. Or with Saskia, whatever. It just filled me with deep peace that she'd have the materials if she wanted them. And if not, so what. I felt better about our lot, and I knew there must have been some grand reason that Craig Luckland had saved me at that construction site that day.

Without quite knowing it, I was coming back to full health. I was washing the dishes, putting away the newspapers in the recycling bin, enjoying the zest of standing back in the world.

One evening, the three of us sat together for the first time in weeks. We quietly pushed spoons into the cartons of orange chicken, ginger chicken, snow peas, and lo mein. It was unlike Joan to pick up take-out for us. Not that she hadn't prepared some beautiful dinners, but the sight of her walking through the door with the grease-stained paper bag stirred me more than I expected. It felt a little like an apology, though what she had to apologize for, I couldn't say.

She lifted the lo mein to her mouth with chopsticks. She kept her eyes mostly on the plate before her, nothing sullen about it, nothing secretive. Her face, if anything, looked serene, more *itself* than it had looked in a week. But I wondered whether I was crushing her with my hopes for a little sign. Not thanks, necessarily; the matter at hand was too complex for that; but I don't know, *some*thing: a finger tapping Morse, a hand splayed and pressed against the tabletop.

Then I wondered whether she'd even seen the folders. I mean, maybe she'd just walked right past them, too much on her mind to take in the desk, the floor, the details of the room. Or was she simply pissed at me for leading her back toward a passion that she'd already said good-bye to? She'd never change the world, she knew it by now, and what is there to say once you recognized that about yourself?

I saw then what I'd been trying not to see: Saskia's hands around her waist, just where her hips started to flare. He smiled and shook his head, looking down in wonderment at the female form.

"This is great, Joan."

Laura smiled, as if she'd forgotten how much she'd enjoyed Chinese food, and the three of us sitting down together as a family, in total ease, no one goofing to cover up any sadness. Or trying too hard to be nice, to mask the inadequacies that lay too deep to see.

"Yeah, you should do this all the time," I said. Tactless, I know.

And what a beautiful opportunity for her to raise her face, to tell me to fuck off. But Joan's smile was small and mysterious. A little knowing. Expertly, she lifted a wet water chestnut to her lips without dropping it to her plate.

I woke up in the middle of the night with the troubling urge to pee. On the way back to bed, I stopped by Joan's room. There was that consoling stripe of light beneath the door, the sound of tapping at her laptop. It was speedy, bright, almost faster than anyone in her right mind could think.

•

Joan lay on the sofa the next morning, blanched, the afghan pulled up to her chin. Her teeth chattered. By now I knew that look too well. It was her turn. I went to the kitchen, placed a cup of water in the microwave and came back with some green tea and a plastic cup of bright orange chemicals (aka flu potion). She didn't want either. She looked up at me, half-swallowed, as if she were afraid I'd bundle her up in a parka and push her out the door to wait for the school bus.

Laura looked especially swift, her arms stretched upward as if she'd been startled at how well she'd slept. Spotting Joan on the couch, she covered her mouth. "Not you, now!"

"The meeting," Joan rasped.

I said, "What about it?"

"I need to be in decent shape for the meeting." And here her voice gave out.

Laura said, "I thought you were taking a break from all that."

Joan looked at me for the first time that day, held my gaze for longer than usual and looked down at her hands clutching the afghan. I had no doubts anymore: I knew this woman. I'd always known this woman.

"When's the meeting?" I said.

"What's today? Where am I?" Joan said, with a high little laugh, giddy and absurd. She smelled of rubber.

"Thursday?" said Laura. That was two days? Yes.

The mightiest sun rays, gold and yellow-green, poured through a parting in the curtains, striking the potted snake plant alive. Immediately, Laura went over to draw the blinds, lest the light bleach out the furniture.

"Don't worry," I said, with a vacant hope that clearly didn't help anyone.

"Don't worry?" Joan laughed with a little gulp in it and burst into the loudest bawling, on and on until the hairs practically rearranged themselves on the back of my shoulders. Her crying would not stop. It scared us in its intensity. It resisted all our dismal attempts to calm her, to make her laugh—just once!—at the racket she was making.

Did Joan know something about us that I didn't know?

Both Laura and I wiped off her tears and led her to the shower. How close she was to falling. She was shot full of fire, a tongue of flame now, working, licking at the walls, the picture frames, the vases, the cracks in the ceiling. I left the room, and Laura peeled down her sister's damp leggings.

Back in our bedroom, I lay diagonally on the bed, stretching out my arms and legs, as if strapped to a wheel. But as hard as I wanted to, I couldn't take up the whole expanse of it. I'd always be small.

•

Somewhere in the land of my past, I stood before the girl who'd sung so beautifully. I hadn't slept well the whole week. I'd woken up every night, thinking about her, but she was distant now, less reachable. I couldn't even see the curve of her lips anymore, the slant of her eyes, the caramel colored flecks in her iris. Sooner or later she'd be tinier than an atom in my memory, and I, in turn, would disappear along with her. I needed to fight myself, lest I give in too easy to that part of me I already hated: the one who'd settle for the drab, easy life at the cost of his soul. Think like that, and before you know it, you're speeding around on your cart on your big fat ass, with nothing to your name but your golf clubs and your busted knees.

Thursday morning. C Wing, between the chemistry labs. The air sweet with waxed floors and janitor's sprays. There Laura was, ten feet away, just when I'd decided I was letting her ruin me, and the kindest thing would be to let her go, to let her fly to Coeur d'Alene for all I cared. But there I was, blocking her way so she couldn't move.

"Excuse me," Laura said.

I stepped to the right. For the first time ever I realized that my forehead came only to her eyebrows and I'd have to do something about that.

She stepped back to the left, and I did the same.

"Yes?" she said.

"I need to have a talk with you." (Elevator shoes? No way: as convincing as a hairpiece or false teeth.)

"I have to get to class." There was the vaguest exasperation in her eyes, but beneath that and inside, something interested, cheered on by the unexpected. I wasn't surprised to see that about her, given what I knew.

"Everything okay here?"

Mitch Cedarbaum, the president of the weightlifters' club, approached like some self-pleased keeper of the peace. In six months of working out his arms and upper body had practically doubled. He made sure to let it be known I didn't exist to him.

Laura closed her eyes, nodding fast. She waved him off like a fruit fly.

"I'd like to go out with you."

She laughed, a quick quizzical laugh, down through her nostrils. If a honeybee could have laughed, that was the sound of it. "I don't even know you."

"Isidore Mirsky," I said, extending my hand.

"Who *are* you?"

But rather than tell her the obvious: that I was in tenth grade and that I lived in a house full of men in the Cambridge Park section of Strathmore, my mind went somewhere else. The question so stumped me that I couldn't speak. Who was I now? A pincer bug? My lips moved uselessly. Which seemed to please Laura Pompoleo no end.

"Okay," she said perfunctorily. She shrugged. "Why not? I'm always up for adventure."

"Really?"

"Yes, really. Where should we meet? I have madrigal practice till four. Then I'm free. Should we go to the boardwalk?"

I said, "I need to tell my friend."

What friend? There wasn't any friend. But I'd needed a friend all of a sudden, so I'd go out and find him. I pushed across the surging stream of people with their backpacks, soccer balls, and calculators in hand, and found a skinny boy turning the combination dial on his locker door. I knew he wouldn't ignore me, because I knew his type too well: no one ever spoke to him.

"If you were ever going on a date, where would you go?" I said.

And how the boy's face gleamed, as if he were certain that I wanted to go out with *him*. "Why don't you just say it?" he said, and blushed. His front teeth glistened as if he'd just brushed them.

"But you're not my type," I said, my head hanging low.

I walked back to Laura without further comment.

"Does he approve?" she said, her head tilted backward, a little superior. And yet she seemed to think my faux pas endearing. Which was more than I could ask for in a woman I knew I'd marry one day.

"Okay," she said. "I'm going to be late. Here's my phone number."

Later that day I ran around the circular track behind the school. I ran and I ran until I collapsed on the grass, winded, nearly sick with my hopes, a stitch in my side by my kidneys. Even Mr. Caicedo, who'd never so much as looked at me during the entire year I sat in his biology class, asked me if I wanted to run cross country. "I have a place for you," he said. And I enjoyed the look on his face when I turned him down with incredible self-possession, or at least the aura of it.

Not long after that I was working out twice, sometimes three times a day, even though Laura insisted that she preferred wiry, sensitive men—Puerto Ricans, Dominicans, Colombians, and Cubans—with both life and death in their eyes.

•

Although her temperature had fallen to a reasonable 98.8, Joan was far from better. She spent the next two days in bed, only getting up for the bathroom or to sit up on the sofa for her mango gelatin. I couldn't look at her face without thinking of my own sickness of last week, and though it was irrational and unfair of me, I resented her for not taking better care of herself, for keeping the sense of threat alive. Was it too much to want health in our house? I was sick of bunched-up Kleenexes and thermometers in view, bottles of aspirin and flu medication: drowsy, non drowsy, tablet, gel caplet, and liquid form. Of course it made perfect sense to me that someone might want to wear a face mask all the time, or wipe down his hands with liquid alcohol. I'd made fun of such people in the past, thinking them too cautious for the real life of sex, contact, and trouble.

I walked in the living room to check on her. Joan lay on the couch with an arm thrown over her face, a posture both carefree and desperate at once.

At least I wasn't flailing about in holy lust.

But the meeting, the meeting. Nothing had been said about the meeting since our conversation regarding it, and it saddened me that she'd be too sick to go. She'd regret that from here on out. She'd kick herself for not getting dressed, for closing her eyes and giving in, giving up. But was it wrong of me to confess to relief? I didn't feel so good about the outcome. Those developers were slick, and I couldn't bear to see her defeated again, and those pro-development forces pecking after her like joyous crows.

Outside the window, I glimpsed the impatiens from the house of my crime. They wilted now. I went out to water them, and the parched soil at their roots took in everything I'd poured.

Sometime later that afternoon, Joan sat up on the couch. She was fully dressed, in the most sensible, office-friendly outfit: black pants, black blouse, black jacket. Her collar was turned up on one side, and I would have walked over and fixed it myself had I not known what was on her mind.

"You're serious," I dropped into the opposite chair with such force that I wouldn't have been surprised to have broken through it, looking up at her with my sore tailbone on the floor.

"I'm feeling somewhat better now." Though she didn't sound terribly convinced, as if the admission threatened her and she'd become delirious.

"*Some*what?"

"Yes."

"And you think you're going to speak before the crowd in that condition?"

"We'll see," she said, followed by a large intake of air. She paused for several strung out seconds, bafflement tensing her brows. She looked at me dead on. "Thank you," she said softly, with a frank stare.

"For what?" And I held onto my ignorance with such conviction that I could look at the Blatherwicks' impatiens out the window without thinking of what I'd done.

"Could you drive me there? I don't think I can drive."

The clock chinked on the wall, minute hand jerking as if it weren't quite sure it was loose enough to move. "The meeting's two hours from now."

"I know that."

"And you're going to sit where you are for a whole two hours?"

She nodded, a parched smile around her lips. "I'm going to concentrate, really, *really* concentrate, on feeling powerful and strong."

"Oh, GOD," I cried, and threw up both my hands over my head and shook them. I had it in me to stomp around the room, to shake the pilings like a lumberjack, but I decided to restrain myself, for the last thing we needed was another opera.

"Enough!" she said, not with rage, but with a cool controlled quiet that could murder.

And that was the word. Out the front window Mr. and Mrs. Seminario, our new neighbors, strolled down the street, arm and arm. They stopped to watch an egret take one step and another across the inklings of a pothole in the road.

•

Joan was still sleeping forty-five minutes before the meeting, and it was oh so tempting not to wake her, to go back to the bedroom and fall into a deep logy state myself. I wasn't entirely over my flu. Still a lingering scratchiness about the throat, and I needed to watch it, lest I get sick again. An hour earlier Laura had called with a report that she wouldn't be home in time for dinner. She and Madison needed to check in a long lost shipment of CDs delivered by Nicolai, the UPS guy, just as she was ready to lock the door for the night.

I said, "Do you know she intends to go to the meeting?"

"*Who?*"

"Joan!" And I said it with such force that it must have carried to the living room. Joan moaned in response, from the next room, thinking I was summoning her when she barely had the strength to sit up in bed.

"Am I surprised?" Laura said quietly. "Of course I'm not surprised." Over the line I heard a shudder, something violent—a box torn open?—followed by a small yelp. Someone had nicked herself on a knife. Or worse. "Could you tell her I'll be there when I'll be there? Where will I find you?"

"Are you okay over there?"

"Where, Isidore."

"Front and center."

"Front and center," she repeated, with a little soft cheer back in her voice. "Listen, handsome, we're beyond busy here. I have to get back to work." Then she'd hung up.

For some odd reason, I replayed that exchange over and over in my head. There was nothing exceptional about that exchange, nothing new. But I let it knock around my head for a little bit. It played itself out like a country song, lonely, wonky, with the twang of the dobro, made to be played late at night, in a truck slashing through cornfields.

My eyes fixed to a ledge of grit on the baseboard. I wiped it off with my index finger and almost put it to my mouth.

I walked out to the living room, where I switched on the lamp. I felt a little spasm, as if I'd be expected to address the crowd in Joan's place. What if it came to that? "Time to go," I said, pushing Joan's arm. I put some weight behind it, with the hope that I could still pin her with the tidy force of a wrestler.

•

I'd like to say that the people outside the building looked as lovely as the last time; that they shared homemade chocolate cupcakes, lit each other's cigarettes. Instead, their fears had made them wary of one another. Some moved through the throng like fins cutting through water. Everyone had a certain sharky quality, which made me that much more fearful for our side, for *Joan*. She just didn't have her armor on—how could she?—and oh how sweet the blood of the weak tastes, especially when you're out to have fun.

It didn't help matters that I'd glanced at an article in the local paper just as we were getting ready to leave. I stood at the kitchen table, while she puzzled over which jacket to wear.

DUNBARTON TOWNSHIP: FIVE CHARGED IN ATTACK ON HOMELESS MAN

Five seniors at Toms River High School have been charged with se-verely beating a homeless person after telling the police that they went "bum hunting" because it was "just something to do." In an attack last Friday, fifty-two year-old Stan Laskin, who lives in the woods off Route Nine, suffered five broken ribs, a punctured lung, and a fractured arm in an attack with pipes and tire irons. Bradley VanderKloot, eighteen, of Toms River, was charged on Tuesday night with aggravated assault and released on $50,000 bail. Four seventeen-year-old males whose names were not released were also charged.

"You okay?" I asked Joan.

She didn't answer. Her head tipped back in the way of the nearsight-ed, when they're trying to see something distant. Even in the waning light—the days were longer now: daylight saving time—I saw her con-tacts, miraculously centered on her corneas.

"What are you looking for?"

Tired question of course, especially when I knew the answer. But Richard, Amy, and even Saskia—now what was up with *that*?—were not a part of the crowd.

We walked inside and sat with our heads down in the front row. I knew she was saving herself, so no talk between us. Familiar faces walked past us—Bess Helen Graver, Honey Wright, Ginger Sadkin—but they made sure not to acknowledge our presence, as if even the possibility of hello would invite conversation, which could possibly invite division, and no one wanted division, not really. Keep it clean and keep it safe, and maybe everyone would get what they wanted, and if that meant some townhouses in the mix, then, you'd better get used to it. For what else was life if not compromise? said these faces. No place for the pure, and what of the past with its fading, antique beacons? The past had never given us anything, so, they'd decided, it was best that we look forward, that we keep our heads held high and be grateful for what's

The new life, ruthless and hungry, was only just beginning. How I already heard it from the sidelines: chewing up the grass, the trees, the shingles off the roofs.

As the chairman stood behind her gavel, Richard and Amy stole through the back door. I signaled Joan's shoulder with a tap, but as she turned around, both of them looked away with tightness in the brow. They'd certainly had enough of her kind, and had hoped she'd stay put, silent, where she belonged.

The madame chairman wasted no time. She seemed to be in a much better mood than the last meeting; it was reflected in a new look: bobbed red hair cut to honor and soften her face. (I hadn't realized till now how much she'd resembled the portrait of George Washington behind her.) She called up two people who more or less repeated what they'd said fourteen days ago ("We didn't spend a half million dollars on our property not to flush our toilets as much as we want") and the chairman cut them off in due time. It made me like her somewhat, no matter whose side she was on. Because she could have let them go on the whole night, because they could have kept circling back to the same, same sentences while the audience grew increasingly jittery to the point where we would have accepted mass murder just to get out of there.

I glanced up. Two uniformed policemen stood to my left, looking directly at me. I rubbed the soles of my shoes back and forth on the carpet, as if cleaning them of mud. When I looked up, they were still looking at me, not with overt suspicion, but with curiosity, as if they'd never seen the likes of my kind before.

I tried to tell myself that such reactions were typical toward me: I was the one who was drawn aside at customs every time I left and entered the country. The size of my nose, the thickness of my brows, and my jaw: already darkish with stubble within two hours of shaving. At least this was how Laura had tried to explain it to me. What's the matter, I don't look like an American? I said back. What about me isn't American? She'd tease me then, telling me my mother had gotten around, that I was part Arab, part African, part gypsy. But in truth, I liked stirring things up, especially in people of that sort. The cops looked at me as if they could actually see the folders in my hot, hot hands, and there I was, down on the foyer floor, pinching up crumbs of potting soil.

I tapped my hand on Joan's knee, just to let her know that we weren't alone, no matter what happened to us.

Testimony continued. Two men and a woman, environmentalists, well-meaning and smart. Facts and figures about least terns, goldfinches, great blue herons, box turtles, and brown-banded wentletraps. I tried my best to look attentive, to keep my shoulders back, despite the lousy, butt punishing chairs, but I couldn't stop thinking about those portraits to my left, which tempted me to stare in their sexless direction. The environmentalists walked back from the podium, not quite convinced that they'd done what they'd set out to do. Then the developer came up. Well, another of his representatives came up. It was strange to note the difference between last time and this time. Without the maps, charts, visuals, whatever, he had nothing to give or say. We felt his weakness right away. We could hear it in his voice, which was loud, peppered with defense. He lost his place at one point, looking left, as if the answer were to be found on the grounds outside, under the trees. When he told off the couple in the third row for whispering, he got it right back. With a terse smile, the chairman told him that that was her job. The people seemed to enjoy that, to enjoy watching someone who, two weeks before, was so confident and slick that he could have tricked us into buying golf course lots in Uganda. Joan looked over at me for the first time since we'd been seated with an expression that said, *maybe there's the slightest bit of hope*, and I wanted to close it right now, for fear she'd be devastated again. That I didn't think we could handle.

Instead, I asked her, "How do you feel?" And I almost enjoyed saying it in full voice to defy the pruney gasbag at the front of the room. Not to mention the policemen who hadn't taken their eyes off me, with the exception of glancing at the clock, or at the pretty woman sitting to my right.

Her turn. It happened so fast that I hadn't prepared myself to feel it, this leavening, as if yeast were rising in me.

She put her shoulders back, she looked at the crowd.

She was new: there was no mistake about it. Somehow the sickness had brought out the best in her: it was something she had to resist, to fight off with every word. I'd never seen her so focused. She seemed to take pleasure in the way her words moved, no pause between them, and she didn't even bother to glance at the notes she'd brought along. She'd remembered figures, facts, pertinent examples; she never went off message. She leaned inward toward the microphone, not arrogant or superior or in any way self-impressed, but intimate and confiding, as if saying, listen, I have something to tell you. And they listened, not because they actually believed that the island should remain undeveloped, or that they should put up with compromised septic tanks until a better solution was at hand, but because they took pleasure in the performance. It was as if a singer had come to town, if one could actually make musical phrases out of reason. I thought of the first time I'd seen Laura on the stage, and I thought of the confident woman standing before me, and the two fused together in my imagination, and God, my God, there they were: a kind and shining sun that blasted out every ugliness in the room. My women! Joan walked away from the stage, and I actually saw a woman to my left start to clap, before she folded her arms across her chest, realizing it wasn't the time or place. She leaned forward, pushed out her lip, as if it were hard to restrain what she knew to be rightful and true.

Then Joan shuddered a little in her seat, and just by looking at her face, I could see her fever. She'd held it off with such presence of mind that it was coming back at her now, to humble her, to let her know that she'd never been in charge. I grabbed for her hand; who cared if anyone saw? I just grabbed it harder, slumping in the seat, pressing my bare arm against hers so I could feel her come in and up through me, candling me.

Were we surprised when the vote went in our favor, four to three? It seemed that we were too blasted to listen to anything after her, not even Richard and Amy, who must have put in a good and decent enough job, but I was too much entertained by the way their eyes kept drifting to Joan, who now had something to give them. They were acknowledging her, repeatedly, in front of the crowd. But as convincing as they must have been, they'd still fallen inside the all-encompassing sweep of her shadow. If the crowd listened, it was only because they'd already gotten the point and liked hearing again what they'd already heard better.

In the parking lot, there was much liveliness and fizz. I wouldn't have been surprised to see champagne corks popping, froth pouring down the sides of bottles to be captured in glasses. Who had ever wanted townhouses, anyway? Give that weedy island back to the birds! And of course there must have been those who drove off with their tires screaming, but the ones who stayed behind seemed to want to catch Joan's eyes. They wanted to let her know, good job, thank you, without holding on to her, or insisting that she'd recognize them.

As for Hazel Luce: she stood among the crowd, smoking a cigarette, feigning detachment, as if she'd just lost a chess match, and was trying to seem a good sport. Anyone in her right mind would know we hadn't seen the last of her.

I put my arm around Joan's shoulder and led her to my truck.

"Joan," someone called behind us. "Joan?"

Ginger Sadkin had her head down, nervous and eager.

"Yes?" The first and only word to come out of Joan's mouth since she'd left the podium.

"Thanks," she said anxiously, and nodded. "You were on tonight. Extremely sharp. Poised. Intelligent." I could tell that praise like that didn't come naturally for her, and it was expected that we appreciate her effort. Then she turned and walked back to her husband, who waved to us with his usual blasé expression.

Outside the truck, my phone rang. Laura! Sweet, ever-reliable Laura! Right on time. Actually, so much had been going on, it hadn't occurred to me that she hadn't come down front and center to sit between us.

"Guess what? No townhouses! Joan nailed it. We won, dear! We absolutely knocked them out of the room!"

"That's great," she mumbled. There was a sound of a drawer sliding open and the jingle of keys dropped. The TV? "Would you mind coming home right now?"

"What's wrong?" I felt the skin around my eyes go loose. I turned my back to the crowd and started walking, phone mashed to my ear, to the trees at the edge of the lot. At the schoolyard beyond that, moths spun and swerved beneath security lights.

"I need you home, okay? Do you think Joan could find her own way home tonight?"

"Of course. Of course. Should I stop and get you anything? Food? Aspirin? Something to drink?"

"Not now," she said. "I'd like you to be with me just now." There was a pause, a space inside the signal. The drawer sliding closed, utensils wrenched. Or were those the keys?

"Sit tight, honey. Stay exactly where you are. I'm coming."

Did I tell Joan? I suppose I did, and I suppose she told me to get home as soon as I could, but those minutes are still lost to me.

What is there to say of lost minutes?

We want to get them over with; we want to hold on to them as long as we can.

I got in the truck. I reached for the key. I reached for the gearshift, slugged it in reverse. I looked over my shoulder. I backed up. I backed up without hitting any parked car, any living creature, any man-made thing. I pulled out into the road. I drove expertly down the road. I never crossed the yellow line in the center of the road. I never rode anyone's tail; I never leaned on the horn with my palm. When the light turned red, I didn't even sweat or curse or bang my hands on the top of the wheel. I gave the truck some gas and drove down the highway like a person, a responsible *citizen*, with someone crucial to attend to.

If something was truly wrong, I'd be frantic, right? I'd feel it all the way from Laura to me like voltage. I'd *taste* it.

Inside my fillings, inside the scab on the back of my wrist.

Ahead, a line of police cars along the road. Blue lights flashing, a lunar emergency of lights. A car inside a stand of trees, front end aiming at the south-bound lane. Steam rising. Though no one seemed to be terribly alarmed. A woman talked to the cops with an outstretched arm, with all the laziness of a deadpan comic trying out a failing routine. One of the cops laughed. The traffic light went green.

And then I drove on.

*

I called her name. I called her name once more. I walked from living room to Joan's room to kitchen. Garage to back deck to bathroom to bedroom. Front yard to side yard and back through the living room. What a lovely story that had brought us all here. Lucky house! The lights! To think I'd been allowed to be a part of it.

On the day of her death, Mama stood on the dock out back. One fish shocked by and then another. She'd never seen such fish in her life: freckled and deep green; certainly they'd escaped from other waters. But when she stepped closer to get a better look, down, down she went, the back of her head banging the raft. And just as she stopped thrashing and pulling and started to sink, she had a thought: *The crime of it. This business of death—bloody and murderous as being born all over again. That's when you should get the cake and the candles. That's right: your name in big black letters on a water tower.*

Attached to the lampshade on the end table, a Post-it note:
I went to Denise's down the street. Don't do that to me ever again. I love you, L.

Then I sat down for one hour with my head in my hands.

CHAPTER 11

I was walking home from work months later when it stopped me: a voice so pure and calm, I didn't know what to do with it.

I couldn't move. I let what I heard come onto me, into me.

The trees took on a shocked raw green, though we were weeks and weeks past spring.

Where did sound like that come from? How did it get made? It wasn't like music on the radio. Nothing about it was that smooth. This voice was too imperfect and alive. It didn't quite make the top notes it was reaching for. The held notes petered off into nothing or went flat. Sometimes this voice even changed keys mid-phrase—or dodged keys altogether, as if rules of that sort were irrelevant or plain nonsense. Not that the voice didn't want you to come along with it. But if the ride should be too unsettling and strange for you? Well, that was your problem. It held onto too much life to be worried about what you thought, because, really, it had too many places to go.

Would you believe me if I told you I didn't know it was Laura right away? I hadn't heard her sing in so long that she sounded like someone else to me. Frankly, it would have been easier to take if the singer had been someone else. I could have kept pretending that it was harmless, that the song had not one thing to do with us, or how we'd turn out.

But think of it, a woman, in the middle of the day, in the middle of her life, puts two hands on the base of her back, opens her throat, and sings aloud to an empty garden, thinking there's no one out there to hear her. So she lets go and gives voice to everything coming at her: the love on the way, the love left behind. And good health. The possibilities. What more could a good man want? And how very nice for the weary traveler, who's had enough of the same old thing, who could stand a little refreshment every now and then.

ABOUT THE AUTHOR

Paul Lisicky is the author of *Lawnboy* and *Famous Builder*. His work has appeared in *Ploughshares, Story Quarterly, Five Points, The Iowa Review, Subtropics,* and *Gulf Coast,* and has been widely anthologized. His awards include fellowships from the National Endowment for the Arts, the James Michener/Copernicus Society, the Henfield Foundation, and the Fine Arts Work Center in Provincetown, where he was twice a fellow. He has taught in the graduate writing programs at Cornell University, Rutgers-Newark, Sarah Lawrence College, and Antioch Los Angeles. He lives in New York City and on the east end of Long Island, and teaches at NYU.

See his blog at http://paullisicky.blogspot.com.

BOOKS FROM ETRUSCAN PRESS

ETRUSCAN IS PROUD OF SUPPORT RECEIVED FROM:

Wilkes University

Youngstown State University

The Raymond John Wean Foundation

The Ohio Arts Council

The Stephen & Jeryl Oristaglio Foundation

The Nin & James Andrews Foundation

National Endowment for the Arts

The Ruth H. Beecher Foundation

The Bates-Manzano Fund

Council of Literary Magazines and Presses

The New Mexico Community Foundation

Founded in 2001 with a generous grant from the Oristaglio Foundation, Etruscan Press is a nonprofit cooperative of poets and writers working to produce and promote books that nurture the dialogue among genres, achieve a distinctive voice, and reshape the literary and cultural histories of which we are a part.

etruscan press
www.etruscanpress.org

Etruscan Press books may be ordered from:

Consortium Book Sales and Distribution
800-283-3572
www.cbsd.com

Small Press Distribution
800-869-7553
www.spdbooks.com

Etruscan Press is a 501(c)(3) nonprofit organization.
Contributions to Etruscan Press are tax deductible
as allowed under applicable law
For more information, a prospectus,
or to order one of our titles,
contact us at books@etruscanpress.org